The Chronicles of Edwin Snipe

To Timothy, Emma, Henry and Lucy with love

The Chronicles of Edwin Snipe

Linda Mann

Priory Press

Published by Priory Press Ltd
The Priory, Abbots Way, Abbotswood,
Ballasalla, Isle of Man IM9 3EQ
www.priory-press.co.uk

ISBN 978-0-9551510-2-6

Typeset by
Frances Hackeson Freelance Publishing Services,
Brinscall, Lancs
Printed in Great Britain by
Cromwell Press, Trowbridge, Wiltshire

Linda Mann worked in the offshore finance sector for ten years until settling on the Isle of Man where she is now married with three children. She was a member of the Isle of Man Arts Council and Chairman of the Film and Literature panel for four years but she now concentrates on writing and trying to keep ahead of the weeds.

She has written for radio and was one of the writers involved with Manx Radio's satirical news programme 'The Headlines Again'.

Books by Linda Mann

The Tavistock Allan Mystery series
Mist
The Tidemaster
The Corsican Trap

The Mr Boots series
Mr Boots

The Edwin Snipe series
The Chronicles of Edwin Snipe

Although this book is set in and around the United Kingdom and there really is an island called the Isle of Man, all the characters and some of the locations are purely fictitious and any similarity to anyone living or dead is simply coincidence and the product of the author's overworked imagination.

Acknowledgements

With many thanks to Francis Charlton for kindly agreeing to read the finished manuscript and for admitting on tape that he liked it.

To Frances Hackeson for the calm and professional production of yet another book and for all her help and ideas.

To Victoria Harrop who stood on a wet towpath during a family holiday in order to get the perfect cover photograph complete with duck … and to her husband and children who let her!

To all politicians everywhere who make my job of lampooning their results so much easier …

And lastly to Messrs Gordons of London who continue to make a very good gin.

Written this year of our Lord 2030

chapter one
Oil

The problem with shagging the Minister for Home Affairs is that by Friday the proverbial cupboard is bare and somebody has to go to the shops and it's usually me.

This particular Friday we had run out of baby oil, scented candles and clean sheets.

"Mark!" I shouted into the well of the bathroom as the high-pressure shower hissed and spat in the corner. The wretched thing had a mind of its own and an almost intelligent method of lulling you into a warm mist, before either scalding your balls off, or freezing your tool of employment to the size of an underage Tesco chipolata.

"What?" Mark grumbled, bent almost double in the miasma of curling vapour. An arm emerged damply from the fog and groped blindly for a pink-fringed towel.

"We're out of oil and candles and the sheets need changing," I growled, at the same time opening the medicine cupboard and peering inside. I rifled carefully through the contents: shaving foam, tin of plasters, three and a half packs of foil wrapped pills marked ‘men only’, moisturiser, antiseptic cream, two half-filled bottles of brown cough syrup, an old bottle of friar’s balsam and an economy size jar of Vaseline.

“Also we’ve got no paracetamol,” I added.

There was a sudden high-pitched scream of anguish, followed by a cloud of steam and something red and shiny erupted from the metal cubicle.

“Why doesn’t someone fix that sodding thing?” Mark spluttered, gingerly touching a throbbing patch of skin on his shoulder.

“Because none of us can wield a spanner. We have other talents, remember,” Harrison Hunt, our newly acquired flat mate remarked, as he oozed into the room and flexed his pectorals at us. He had a brain the size of a pea and a body which when fully inflated, could do walk-ons in ‘Gladiator’, a film I’d got out of the Member’s Library at least three times. It was actually one of the banned classics for the general populace but as we all know, the people that make the rules break the rules. Which just goes to show that although Orwell got 1984 completely wrong, being at least twenty years too early, he did know what he was saying when he wrote that ‘all animals are equal, some are more equal than others’.

My head had now begun to throb to the point of actually wanting to get a gulp of non-reconditioned air, and so, sighing in a somewhat laboured fashion I left the bathroom, picked up my plastic identity wallet and marched out of the flat, taking care to slam the front door as loudly as humanly possible upon departure.

The sky outside, or at least the bit viewed above the collection of rooftops, solar panels and plastic wind turbines was a bright peacock blue. Not a cloud scuttled across its surface and the breeze blowing in from the coast was cool and smelt of old socks and boiled sprouts.

When I finally reached the shopping precinct down by the old docks, I paused to consult my reflection in the chemist's window before entering. The man with the tweed cap was still following.

Inside the cool aluminium and glass interior I located a large pack of cotton buds, half a litre of body oil and two dozen scented candles. They had run out of Camellia so I had to make do with Lavender and Forest Walks. The flat would, I had no doubt, stink like the municipal baths and recreation complex after about an hour but the alternative was switching the lights on and actually seeing what we did for a living and with whom. Candlelight was, after all, extremely kind to the body beautiful and with luck wouldn't show up any newly acquired wrinkles or grey hairs. 'God,' I thought. 'I've become as vain as I remember my grandmother being, during the early part of the new millennium, before the carnage and the New Management.'

I paused at the counter and fishing around for my credit card caught sight of the chap with the cap, hiding behind the shampoo and conditioner. The anaemic-looking youth at the till yawned, showing a metal-filled mouth and scratched a yellow pus-filled spot behind his left ear.

"Anything else?" he asked in the bored tones of the latent adolescent.

"Large pack of paracetamol," I said, finding my Switch card, sandwiched between my leisure entry visa key and my security pass.

"That it?"

"Yes," I replied, trying not to look as the pimple erupted.

"Right that's twenty five and forty Eucs including tax. Do I have permission to debit?" As his finger hovered over the send button on the CamTill, I had a sudden mad urge to say no and walk off but I didn't, I just nodded and grabbed my card and the brown paper carrier bag containing my motley assortment of shopping.

Coffee, I muttered to myself and with a sudden spurt of enthusiasm hurried over to the bookshop opposite and mounted the escalator.

I was just trying to work out whether Fat Andy would succeed in America when the tweed cap sat down opposite me, causing my cafe latte to wobble, the froth lifting over my one indulgence of extra chocolate flakes.

"Oi!" I exclaimed, "Watch it."

"Sorry," he muttered, wiping a not overly clean cotton handkerchief over his copiously perspiring forehead.

"Do I know you?" I asked suspiciously, taking in the old-fashioned frayed and patched clothing and the large red bucolic face. He looked exactly like Farmer Ted, from my old primary school reading books. The page before he stabs the man from the Ministry of Agriculture with a pitch-fork.

"Not exactly," he replied, carefully beginning to extract something from his pocket.

"Look," I hissed, "if you're one of the great unwashed of the gutter press, you can bloody well go through the bins like everyone else. We put them out by the laburnum on a Thursday night. So you've got at least a couple of hours for a quick rummage. Now piss off and leave me alone." I wasn't, I hasten to add, usually this rude but I'd been looking forward to a quiet read and a thoroughly unhealthy coffee all morning.

"Listen to me young Edwin, this is important, it's ..." The voice tailed away as he stared past my left ear. He gave a sort of strangled squawk and then suddenly took off down the stairs, scattering shoppers as he went.

To this day I don't know why I followed him: why I couldn't have shrugged my shoulders and continued reading I will never know. Only I didn't because by then I'd spotted the plain white plastic bag he'd left by the chair and, thinking it was important, hurried after him.

"Stop!" I bellowed as he sprinted sweatily down past Woolworths. "You've forgotten your bag."

He turned then and glared at me, his whole body quivering in that awful hairy jacket.

"What?" he barked back.

"Your bag." I waved the thing at him; it clunked heavily against my leg.

"What bag?"

"This one", I replied as I dropped it on the ground.

"Don't touch it!"

"Why not?" I asked, intrigued.

"Because ..."

What he was going to say next was lost in a sudden ear-splitting roar, as screaming, he burst into a mass of white and gold flames.

I remember dropping my own shopping and watching the bottle of scented oil break and slowly spread, leaving a puddle of reflections around my feet. After that I have absolutely no idea what happened, except that the lights went out and I fell, the feeling of falling staying with me until I awoke, in a strange bed in a strange room with a very strange man looming over me.

chapter two

Ward 10

"Argh!" I screamed. The man leapt back as if I'd shot him and the needle he'd been about to thoughtfully press into some part of my anatomy, fell to the floor with a crash.

There was a flat, warm silence as we glared at each other.

The sudden entrance of a large blue-clad nurse of Amazonian proportions had the strange man scrabbling on the floor not unlike a demented meerkat, as he tried desperately to pick up the little shards of glass. One large sliver winked and gleamed at me from the side of my municipal white laminate locker.

"You missed a bit," I said in a low whisper and pointed helpfully in completely the wrong direction as I carefully pushed the tall utilitarian cupboard over the piece of glass, whilst making a grab for the plastic mug of iced water I could see wedged on its bare polished surface.

By now the blue avenger had arrived at the foot of my bed, breathing heavily and with the fire of superiority burning in eyes as steely blue as her starched uniform. Gold buttons gleamed in the stark blue-white light of the overhead neon tubes. Her face, surmounted by dark hair pinned and plaited into submission could have been used as a geographical map of the Cairngorms. She waited, bosoms heaving beneath the amply filled and immaculately ironed cloth. The man beside me had begun to back away but he was much too slow. For with the speed and agility of a preying mantis she had him pinned down between the locker and the white painted wall before I even had time to blink in surprise.

"And what," she asked in the booming tones of the educated Edinburgh Scot, "do you think you are doing, Mr Warwick?"

"Nothing," he mumbled, turning a deep purply red.

"Sister!" she barked, bosom heaving.

We waited as a small lady in a green uniform scuttled from behind the closed curtains of an end bed and hurried towards us clutching an oval silver-coloured pan, covered with a large piece of kitchen paper. As she approached the mixed aroma of bleach and something meaty reached us.

I sincerely hoped I'd missed lunch.

"Yes Matron?" she asked a trifle timidly.

"What is *that* doing in here on its own?"

"Mr Warwick?"

"Yes Mr Warwick, Sister, if that is his name, which I very much doubt!"

"Oh but …"

"Did I give you permission to speak, you nasty little man?"

"No, but I …"

If it hadn't have been for the fact that I'd caught him trying to inject me with some unknown and probably lethal substance, I might have felt sorry for him – as it was I sat back and took a silent sip of ice-cold water.

"And just exactly what" she added in the tones of one determined to find out, "do you have in your hand?"

I looked at the offending appendage with interest and noticed a small trickle of blood, which had been oozing slowly onto the floor, in short spasmodic drips.

The man, now showing a slight green tinge in the over-powering puce, gave a sickly grin and reluctantly opened his fist, the knuckles white against the stretched skin. A shower of bright sparkling red and silver pieces joined the gently congealing fluid on the floor. Matron glowered at him, every single chin wobbling in undisguised disgust.

"Security!" she bellowed.

The ward that had previously appeared so uncluttered and funereally quiet, was almost immediately bursting at the seams with some of the largest and most fearsome examples of the male orderly I'd ever been privileged to meet. Mr Warwick gurgled something which might have been an apology of sorts and was frogmarched from the room, his feet remaining a good six inches off the ground. Matron watched, her lips pursed in dour approval, and just before they were out of earshot roared, "And you had better give him a tetanus jab." There was a tiny pause before she added, eyes twinkling maliciously, "A large one."

The door at the end of the ward closed inwards as the stifled cries of Mr. Warwick faded to low verminous squeaks of sound.

"Right," said Matron, fixing me with a hard stare. "I believe someone wants a word with you."

I must have looked suitably puzzled because it was with only a tinge of exasperation that she added the words, "The Police."

"The police?" I repeated. "Why?"

"Why indeed?" she barked as she turned and marched off down the ward, her metal-tipped heels clicking loudly with each carefully measured step.

I was still trying to work out why the police would want to talk to me when they turned up. The first was one of the tallest women I had ever seen, the second and elder of the two, one of the shortest men.

The woman introduced herself as Detective Inspector Jo Smallpiece before she moved off towards the end of the ward, where a stack of chairs lay resting against a large damp patch.

She returned and parking her carefully selected plastic cube next to my bed, promptly sat down, and then finding a notepad and pen waited patiently for her companion to stop fiddling with my notes, clipped to the end of my bed and to start the interrogation proper.

I was fascinated by her hands. They were the largest and the best kept I think I'd ever seen. Each nail positively glowed in its immaculate coat of pale pink gloss, each cuticle a perfect half moon.

The man, seeing me staring, coughed. I looked up, muttered 'sorry' and took another sip of water. The ice was now little more than a cold memory at the bottom of the tumbler.

"So you are Mr Edwin Snipe?" he asked, sitting down on the end of the bed.

"Yes," I answered a trifle nervously.

"My name is Sergeant Dave Driscoll and I'd like you to answer a few questions and then when Matron pronounces that you are fit and well, you can answer a whole lot more down at the station. Right?"

"Er, right," I agreed, nodding wildly.

I watched as he stared at the far wall before sucking in his cheeks and fixing me with the kind of benign smile foxes give rabbits just before they decide which one will be lunch.

"Do a lot of shopping, do you?"

"What?"

"Shopping."

"Er ..."

"Only you left a couple of carrier bags in the shopping precinct."

"I only had one bag."

"Well we found two."

"Well one wasn't mine, it belonged to the middle-aged guy in the hairy jacket."

"Hairy jacket?"

"The chap that ..." I stopped, seeing again that sudden burst of white and gold.

"Combusted."

"Sorry?"

"Spontaneous Combustion – not a common form of death."

"No."

"My first."

"Oh." We sat for a while in silence.

"So what exactly made you do it?" he asked.

"Do what?"

"Run amok."

"Do what!"

"Well, according to my notes and the CCTV camera you ran around the precinct completely out of your mind for a good ten minutes with a large tin of lighter fuel and a box of matches."

"I'm sorry, I …"

"We had to shoot you in the end." I must have looked suitably stunned because he added a good deal more kindly. "With a knock-out dart."

"Oh."

"Well?"

"Look officer, all I can remember is this chap in a hairy suit bursting into flames and me dropping my shopping and then waking up to find some strange man called Mr Warwick bending over me with a hypodermic in his hand."

There was a pause as they both digested this.

"So you don't remember anything?"

"No – I told you." I looked from one blank face to the other. Whatever they really thought, neither of them was saying.

"Mr Warwick?" Jo Smallpiece asked, doodling a large dagger in the corner of her notepad. At least I think it was a dagger, although on the other hand it could have been a badly drawn plane.

"Matron caught him and threw him out. You must have passed him on your way in," I explained helpfully. A hangman's noose had now been added to the previous drawing together with a flower made of hearts. Perhaps she had boyfriend trouble.

They exchanged another look and I began to wonder what exactly it was that they thought I knew but that they didn't want me to know that they knew.

"Ah, Mr Warwick."

"Couldn't have happened to a nicer bloke," Dave Driscoll drily tittered. With his grey eyes sparkling, all he needed was a fishing rod and a woolly hat and he could have been right at home in my Aunty Elsie's front garden. I really hadn't got a clue what the joke was about but as it seemed to be keeping them both in a good mood, I politely waited for the inquisition to continue.

"Shock," muttered Dave Driscoll.

"Pardon?"

"Must have been a bit of a shock," he added almost kindly.

"Yes."

"Right, well we'll leave you to the medical profession and when you're feeling a bit better we'll escort you down to the station."

"But I haven't done anything!" I squeaked fearfully.

"Oh I'm sure you'll remember most of it in due course, in any case you can always watch the video."

"Video."

"That's right. Now you just have a nice little rest and a bite to eat and we'll be back just as soon as Matron gives us the go-ahead."

And they then left, just like that, leaving me with the dead feeling of the recently run over. I couldn't remember a thing, not a single solitary thing, so why on earth did I feel so guilty?

chapter three
Mavis Wordsworth

After they had gone, I sat hunched up in my clean white scratchy sheets and tried to think. Independent thought wasn't one of my strong points. I had always previously managed to live quite a happy contented life by pointedly not having to think. With a mother who could have thought for England, it was, generally speaking, the safest option.

I was still deep in panic when the food trolley arrived.

It rattled and groaned its unseen way down the corridor and was then pushed into the ward by a very plain blonde, in a badly fitting uniform. By badly fitting I mean it clung in all the places you'd rather it didn't and hung loosely in all the ones you'd rather it did.

"Well?" she barked at me. "What do you want for lunch?"

"Lunch?" I repeated blankly.

"Lunch. We've got some nice beef in a sort of casserole or there's fish, don't ask me what kind because I don't catch or cook it. Right!"

"Er right," I agreed. "Do you have any salad?" I asked tentatively.

"No."

"Um, I'll have the beef."

"Do you want potatoes?"

"Yes please." After all this was a hospital and there wasn't much you could do with the humble spud.

"Chipped, baked, mashed, sautéed, with cream and onions or cooked with spices and chick peas?"

I was wrong.

"Er, mashed. Any veg?" I asked as a dollop of something white was added to the brown lumps.

"Peas?"

"Please." I received a hard stare and my plate was dumped onto my lap together with a knife and fork. I took a tentative bite. It was really good.

"Pudding?"

"What have you got?"

"There's a treacle sponge or some sort of jelly."

"I'll have the sponge," I muttered through a mouthful of buttery mash. I could get used to this; it was certainly better than my cooking. Even Mark's special pink pasta surprise paled into insignificance. It was something he'd invented with tuna, ketchup and condensed milk. It wasn't that bad really and it wasn't black, which was the most important thing.

I watched with interest as she bent down to unearth the puddings on the bottom shelf. There was, I thought, something really wrong with her hair. For one thing it moved when she didn't and for another there were tufts of brown poking out at the back. I'd almost plucked up the courage to ask why she was wearing a wig, when she straightened up and as she deposited the covered dish on my locker, whispered. "Do you want to get out of here?"

"Er …"

She looked up and down the ward before hissing, "I can get you out for a price."

"Price?" I repeated blankly.

"An exclusive."

I choked, spraying globules of peas and mash across the bed. That was why she'd looked oddly familiar – she was one of them. The gutter press, the enemy. This purveyor of fine food was none other than Mavis Wordsworth the foul-mouthed harridan who'd caused more nervous breakdowns than the Department for Social Affairs.

"You!" I uttered in accents of utter loathing.

"Keep it down," she snarled back.

"Why?" I asked, suddenly guessing the reason behind the nervous sideways looks. "Doesn't Matron know who you really are?"

"Shut up."

"Is that why you're wandering around in one of the worst-fitting uniforms I've ever seen? … And as for that wig!" I laughed outright, beginning for the first time that day to really enjoy myself.

"What's wrong with it?" she asked, plainly upset.

"What's right with it?" I replied, waving a forkful of meat at her.

"It cost nearly a hundred Eucs!"

"You were robbed," I stated, scooping up some more mash.

"Oh." She looked, I had to admit, a bit like a recently kicked spaniel, all big brown eyes and droopy ears.

"Anyway you could always buy it a lead," I said, pointing at her head. "I'm sure someone will give it a good home. Housetrained, is it?"

"You!" she gave me a look which could have stripped paint.

"Matron!" I whispered, bending to my half-empty plate. Hurriedly she grabbed the trolley handle and scooted off towards the end bed. Matron paused in her inspection of the ward and gave me a suspicious look before she too made her imperial way to the end bed, still curtained off and emitting at odd intervals some interesting odours.

I sat in a state of sleepy boredom after finishing my lunch. One of the cleaning staff had switched on the overhead TV. Two men were arguing over the correct way to stuff sprouts and a lady tennis player was holding court over the number of orgasms you could have in half an hour. She had a face like a wet alpaca and a body many of her male contemporaries would have given their backhand swing for.

I was still trying to work out why anyone would want to stuff a sprout when something hissed at me from the end of the bed. It was Mavis and the wig.

"What do you want?" I asked.

"Just wanted to leave you some light reading," she replied silkily, tossing a motley assortment of tabloid newspapers at me.

Before I could think of anything even vaguely witty she'd gone. Carefully I reached down and picked the first one up. A well-known face leapt at me from the front page. Not surprising really as it was mine.

With shaking hands and a heart that had suddenly discovered the quickstep I read the covering story. I had, it alleged, suffered a complete breakdown when one of my close relatives had died in front of me. Crazy with grief I had careered around the shopping precinct spraying passers-by, including a pregnant lady with a two-year-old strapped in a buggy, with lighter fuel. I had then started lighting matches, with which I threatened several octogenarians and the manager of WH Smiths before being shot by a local vet. There were calls for all sorts of social improvements, one of which involved having me castrated and sent to Australia.

In a state of abject terror and a certain amount of disbelief I read the other papers as well. They all said the same thing, more or less, and two of them had pictures. No wonder the police were talking of having a quiet word. According to at least three of the editorials I deserved nothing less than ten years servitude in the more notorious of jails; one even proposed a particularly messy death.

Trembling I sat and contemplated the pages spread over my lap, a sob hovering on my lips.

"So do you want coffee with your hair shirt or tea?"

It was Mavis grinning from ear to ear over the edge of her trolley.

"Get me out of here!" I squeaked.

"One lump or two?" she asked, handing me a cup of what looked like coffee but smelt like tea.

"Please?" I added pathetically.

"Nice touch that, the quivering of the bottom lip but 'please' is not the magic word," she muttered maliciously, before collecting the empty crockery from the top of my locker.

I felt myself being manoeuvred into a corner by an expert. I could hold out but by then I'd be in some brightly lit cell awaiting a few questions with or without electrodes. I swallowed and stifled the small voice which kept repeating Clarris Sharpe's mantra, 'Never talk to the press, never talk …'

"All right," I reluctantly whimpered.

"Exclusive?" she whispered back, her head bent over mine. I gulped loudly, swallowed what little pride I had left and nodded.

"Be ready when they turn the lights out tonight." She turned her back on me and added in urgent tones. "And for heaven's sake hide those papers before Matron sees and reckons if you can read them you can go play with the nice police officers."

"Right," I muttered gathering them up and hurriedly stuffing them under my sheets, where they rustled alarmingly.

I watched as Mavis, my human life preserver, rattled off. It had been a very strange day and it looked like it was going to be an even stranger evening.

chapter four
The great escape

I managed somehow to survive the remainder of the day. I remember carefully folding what felt like acres of newspaper into smaller wads, which I surreptitiously stuffed into the confines of my locker.

At some point Sister descended on me wearing a thin-lipped scowl and took my temperature. I remember almost weeping into the sheets, as I had to crouch, exposed bottom in the air, thermometer clenched between my buttocks. After that she was a little kinder, as according to her, I had a temperature, racing heartbeat and high blood pressure.

A sign was hung over my pillows stating 'No Visitors' in bold black type and the curtains were drawn around my bed. I hid in my little cave-like space and tried to remember what had happened after the man in the hairy jacket exploded.

I couldn't recall a thing.

Finally after what seemed like hours Mavis returned and after delivering a large plate of cheese on toast and a mug of tea, handed me a small white plastic bag, which I hid under my bedclothes.

"What do you want me to do with it?" I asked.

"Blow it up," she replied. "I hear you're really good at that sort of thing."

She gave a nasty laugh and disappeared behind the expanse of curtain.

"Evil-minded cow," I muttered, nibbling on the toast.

When I'd finished I had a quick look at the bag's contents. There was a small brown paper package containing a wig which almost matched my own colouring, and a blow-up doll. I was still trying to fill the arms with air when I heard the trolley return.

Just in case it wasn't Mavis I hid the thing under the sheets and sat on it. It gave a long low hiss and emitted the loudest fart I'd ever heard.

"Was it the cheese?" Mavis sweetly asked as she handed me a mug of cocoa.

"No it bloody well wasn't!" I replied, red with embarrassment.

"Well don't puncture it, I've only got the one."

"Why do I need a wig?" I asked.

"You don't, he does," she muttered, peering around the curtains.

"It's clear." She turned back to me and almost gave me a smile. "In about an hour's time I'll be back with an auxiliary's uniform. Put your gown and the wig on the doll and get into the uniform. Leave the doll in the bed and cover it up. Then we both walk out together."

"Is that it?" I asked. Nothing, I thought, was that simple.

"For now," Mavis stated firmly.

I watched her go and then finished blowing the doll's arm up. I hid it under the bed while I slowly made my way to the end bathroom. There had been a bit of a conversation between Matron and Sister over the non-existence of what they termed my movements. The cheese seemed to have done the trick though and I spent quite a bit of time hunched over the toilet, as the world literally fell out of my bottom. I returned to find Matron reading my notes.

"So," she said, watching me with her all-seeing eyes. "Feeling a little better are we?"

"Yes Matron."

"Good, good." Again there was that narrowed look. "What you need, laddie, is a good night's sleep and then tomorrow we can hand you over to the authorities and get our bed back."

I gulped at the word 'authorities'. Matron, indifferent to my trembling distress, turned on her heel and went back to the distantly-lit nurses station. There was a shout of 'Lights out!' and the world dimmed and reddened.

Quickly I dressed the doll in my gown and wig. I had discovered when hiding the papers that someone had left a bag of my underclothes in my locker and these I carefully put on. It's funny how reassuring the feel of your own boxer shorts and socks can be.

I'd almost given up on Mavis and was half asleep when she suddenly emerged from the folds of garishly flowered curtain material and thrust a pair of white overalls and blue plastic overshoes into my hands.

I managed to put them on in under two minutes and in a state of total funk followed her from the room.

Outside, the brilliantly lit corridor had me blinking rapidly. A long ambulance trolley was parked up against the wall.

"Get on," she hissed.

I did as I was told.

"Play dead," Mavis muttered, throwing a sheet over me. She then grabbed my arm and stabbed a hypodermic needle into my un-relaxed skin. I tried to scream, failed and slid into unconsciousness.

There was a feeling of sleepy well-being as I began to come to; that is until I opened my eyes and stared at the ceiling now three inches above my head. I made my eyes explore further and what they saw, had me quivering like the proverbial jelly. I was in a metal box and it was very cold. I could just about make out a few sounds; one of them was the ticking of my watch. I squinted down at the luminous dial; it was half past one. Although I had no idea if that meant early morning or afternoon. Minutes ticked slowly by.

At two thirty-five the box was opened and the face of Mavis loomed over me.

"Sorry," she muttered, nervously looking around. "There was a bit of trouble, a car crash, people everywhere."

I nodded.

"Come on, out you get."

She pulled and I somehow managed to extricate cold and shaking limbs from the confines of what I could now see was a metal drawer. I was in a large dimly lit room, which smelt strongly of bleach and fresh paint.

"Come on," Mavis urged, thrusting a brown suit at me.

The tag on the lapel said 'John Mishkin. Path Ass.'

"Where?" I asked.

"No time," she replied, steering me towards the door. Behind me one of the drawers quivered and a small voice shouted, "Help!"

We walked quickly down a long tunnel-like corridor,

swathed in multi-coloured pipes, our footsteps ringing loudly, as we hurried along the bright red, painted, concrete floor. Finally we emerged through a plastic sheet covered swing door, into a green walled oasis. The air smelt of roses and honeysuckle and I think it was quite possibly the loveliest oxygen I had ever breathed.

"Come on, hurry," Mavis muttered as she began to look furtively to the left and right. Finally satisfied that we were not being observed, she opened a heavy green metal door in the wall and pushed me through. We were now in a vast orange-lit car park full of a large selection of brightly painted little cars. Mavis made her way to the far end where an old green Skoda lurked and jumped into the driver's seat.

I fumbled with the passenger door and clambered in just as she started the engine and threw the thing into reverse. I sat in silence, hunched down in the passenger well, a coat of Mavis's barely covering me, as we carefully negotiated the maze of sleeping policemen and brick ramps. We eventually left the car park and drove off past rows of terraced houses and neatly manicured gardens, their owners safely slumbering behind ruched and scalloped nets.

I must have fallen asleep because I woke with a jolt as a garage door clattered into place and a large hand pummelled my shoulder.

"What now?" I whimpered, looking up. Blue eyes gazed down at me and I gasped in stunned surprise.

"Dad?" I stuttered, before passing out again.

chapter five

Bill and Ben

I came to again, just as I was being manoeuvred up a twisting flight of wrought iron steps. As soon as my eyelids flickered I was gently dumped, a terse conversation continuing over the top of my head.

"Just exactly how much of that stuff did you pump into him?"

"Enough."

"If I'd known …"

"You'd have done what exactly?"

"Well …"

"We could have got him out ourselves."

"Oh sure, and Matron would have allowed you free range, eh?"

"No one would have suspected a pair of orderlies."

"Look, do you honestly think you would have got past the police or Warwick?"

"Warwick." There was a pause before I heard a sigh and someone sat down next to me.

"I thought ..."

"No you didn't and that's the problem, nobody does think. This isn't a game any more. I would have thought that after what happened to Toby, you would both have realized that."

"It wasn't our idea to involve the boy."

"Or mine. Do you honestly think I relish the prospect of involving some naive political pet?"

Outraged and feeling slightly drunk I tried to stand. The movement made them all aware that I was at least alive and half pushed from one side and pulled from the other I was finally deposited on a large rug-covered sofa.

"Do you want anything Edwin?" my father asked.

"Yes, a large cup of tea and half a bottle of aspirin," I replied, trying to shake the fog out of my head.

Almost immediately a mug of tea was put in front of me and two white round tablets were shaken into my still trembling hands.

"Look, he's still shaking," my father pointed out, clearly upset.

"It'll wear off in about half an hour – it's just a reaction. All he needs is food and sleep."

"And an explanation," I muttered, sipping my tea. The aspirin had melted on the way down leaving an unpleasantly bitter aftertaste.

"I'll make us all some breakfast," said the third voice. I looked up and saw a small round man with a short beard and one of the loudest jumpers I'd ever seen outside a production of 'Josephine and the Amazing Technicolor Dream Coat'. I was still trying to work out why anyone would want to knit fuscia pink next to acid yellow and mint green when he kissed my father on the cheek, patted his bottom and moved away. I looked up and met my father's steady gaze. So that was Ben the home-breaker, the man who had taken my beloved father away when I was four and a half. The man I'd plotted and planned against in my mind, for years.

"So that was Ben," I stated, my voice carefully neutral.

"Yes."

"Oh." There wasn't really much else I could politely say.

"You mean you've never met?" Mavis asked, settling herself cross-legged on the floor.

"No," my father and I both said at the same time.

"Oh." Mavis looked slightly nonplussed and grabbing a cushion from the chintz-covered chair behind her, began to plait its braided fringe.

"He's shorter than I imagined," I said, trying to come to terms with meeting the adult equivalent of the big bad wolf.

"I love him," my father gruffly stated, before sitting down in the armchair opposite and staring at me in the sort of way Mark would stare at a cream cake. It was that same desperate combination of wanting and fear. Wanting to eat it and the fear that if he did he'd develop spots – or worse – a bulge in his fabulously flat stomach.

"More than me?" I asked, the old resentments finally finding voice.

"No! Not more than you. I love you just as much, maybe more. It's different."

He got up and began to pace the floor. Mavis and I sat and watched him circumnavigate the room several times before he turned and faced us.

"You left me," I said, trying to keep the bitterness out of my voice and failing big time.

"I didn't want to."

"Then why did you go?" I asked, all the old hurt

contained in a single word. That single word 'why?' The word that had haunted me for nearly twenty years but now I had the chance to ask it, I had the traitorous feeling deep inside, that I really didn't want to know.

"I couldn't stay. The arguments were tearing me apart. I wanted to take you with me but …"

"Don't you dare blame mother!" I shouted.

"I wasn't going to, I …"

"Blame me if you have to blame someone. I didn't want him to bring you and …" The jumper placed a plate of bacon and eggs in front of me. I stared at it, as if it were poisoned.

"Eat," begged my father.

"I don't want it." My voice even to my own ears sounded more like a sulky nine-year-old than a grown man. "I don't want anything from him!"

"It's not Ben's fault," my father argued.

"He took you away."

"No."

"Because you didn't love me anymore."

"That's not true. Your mother …"

"Don't blame her – she never said anything." That was true and perhaps with hindsight it would have been better if she had.

"Well, if you're not going to eat that …" Mavis moved towards my plate and as she did I suddenly felt ravenously hungry.

"Oh no you don't," I muttered mutinously and began to eat. It was good and the bread that I mopped the egg up with was perhaps the best I'd ever tasted. Then I remembered Ben was a chef.

"So that's why you left," I observed ruefully as I laid my

knife and fork to rest.

"Why?"

"Because Ben can cook and mother used to burn gravy."

My father sat and stared at me and then began to laugh, tears rolling down his face and settling in wet globules on the neck of his yellow polo shirt.

"Well," Mavis declared, looking at the pair of us. "I'm glad that's settled because I don't suppose there's any chance that I might get something to eat too. After all I am the one that rescued the prodigal son from the jaws of death."

As if on cue Ben arrived back in the room with two more plates of food and a large jug of coffee. I helped myself to more bread and a mug of black nectar whilst Mavis and my father tucked in. Ben stood with arms folded and watched. Looking up, I caught him staring at me. His gaze was one of muted resentment. I knew how it felt and to be honest I was actually rather pleased.

"So," I asked, settling back and cradling my mug of coffee in my hands, "who exactly is Mr Warwick and why would the police believe that I knew that poor chap who blew up?"

Mavis and my father exchanged worried looks after which there was a long thought-filled silence broken finally by Ben of all people.

"I think the lad deserves an explanation, don't you Bill? After all he could be the next one on their list."

"List! What list?" I squeaked.

It had been bad enough getting caught up in a violent death but now it seemed that not only was the first death deliberate but that somehow it involved not only myself but my father and one of the nastier scions of the reporting world. I glared at Mavis and my father; they obviously knew each other and had done for some time and even more unnerving than that was the unpalatable fact that they also appeared to be friends!

chapter six

My Uncle Tobias

"Well," my father began, nervously looking at Mavis. She gave him a stony look in return, before taking up her interrupted plaiting. "I suppose I should explain who your Uncle Tobias is."

"Was," Mavis softly interjected without raising her eyes from the long silken strands she was mutilating.

"Yes. Was."

There was a pause while he pursed his lips in concentration and frowned down at his mug of slowly cooling coffee. Ben, plainly irritated, expelled air with a whale- like snort and tossed a small sepia brown print at me. Although the man in the photograph was a lot younger, he was, even without the hairy suit, undoubtedly my human torch.

"Oh for heaven's sake how difficult can it be?" he muttered. "That," he said, plonking himself next to me and prodding the photo with a podgy ring-covered index finger, "was your Uncle Tobias."

"Then why have I never heard of him?" This was a reasonable enough question even to my oversensitive ears. The reaction of the other three, however, was one of acute embarrassment.

"Well the thing is, we – that is your mother and I – sort of lost contact with him before we got married. Then what with all the turmoil of the millennium riots we believed he was dead."

"Why?" I asked, completely lost.

"Tobias was your father's older and much more brilliant brother," Ben interrupted crossly. "Your father had a row with him because he found your mother and your uncle in bed together the week before they were going to get married. Tobias told Louise, your mother, that Bill was gay. Your mother said she knew but that she was pregnant and was going to marry Bill anyway because she didn't approve of the work he, Tobias, was doing."

"What work?" I asked.

"Some form of biochemistry. Very hush hush. He worked at a place called Portland Down. It was burnt down during the riots and we all assumed that he was one of the three hundred-odd reported dead. That is, until Mavis turned up here, asking questions about him," my father replied uneasily.

"Hang on a minute," I said, a horrible thought hitting me right between the eyes.

"What – do you mean mother was pregnant and sleeping with this Tobias character? You mean mother was sleeping with both of you?" I asked, deeply scandalized. It was bad enough knowing that your parents had had sex in the first place without wondering if they'd got up to the sort of things you did yourself.

"Er, no," my father reddened considerably and refused to look at me.

"And just what exactly does 'Er no' mean?" I asked, my voice icy.

"Your mother slept with your uncle and your father is not your biological ..." Ben's voice tailed away, as I gave him my best drop-dead-immediately look.

"Are you trying to tell me that some sad-looking bucolic mad scientist with an appalling taste in clothes is actually my dad?" There – I'd finally admitted it.

"Yes," came the reply from three sides of the room.

"Oh," I muttered. My brain began to do all sorts of pondering as it viewed the ramifications of all this, the main one being that for some reason I was relieved. Perhaps deep down I'd always wondered if being gay was hereditary. I suspected that Mark and Harrison had because I'd caught them giving me funny looks when they were in the bathroom and I'd toddled in to borrow something, usually clean towels. Ben grinned at me and patted my thigh. Were my thoughts that obvious? If so, I could see myself buying a large plastic mask. Carefully I inched away on the pretext of pouring myself more coffee.

"Well that certainly explains a few things. What it doesn't explain is how you know the crusading word 'vivisectionist'," I asked, glaring pointedly at Mavis, who in my now newly informed view was definitely the last person I wanted at a family laundry session.

"Um ..." was the reply.

"I know this sounds crazy but the answer 'um' doesn't exactly go with your usual poisonous journalistic ramblings," I snapped, glaring at her.

"Er ..."

"How about if I ask a few questions and you concoct a few standard replies?" I asked in tones of great sweetness.

"I couldn't possibly comment," she replied.

"And now she's stealing all my best lines. Dad," I pleaded, "will you please tell me what this has got to do with her and why am I on a list?"

My father glanced worriedly at Ben who shrugged and settled back further into the sofa. I actually got the distinct feeling he was beginning to enjoy this. Frankly although I hated to admit it, in his position so would I.

"Your Uncle Tobias has been working in a secret department very few people know exists and it isn't one that the government will ever admit to having."

I sighed; well that was Clarris Sharpe my bed playmate and boss out of the interrogation loop, as everybody from the refuse operatives and upwards know that the last person who is told anything is the minister in charge.

"Your uncle was working on some secret formula, something to do with ultraviolet light. However about a year ago something went wrong. There was another explosion and I think Toby finally realized just exactly what he could be dealing with. So he disappeared. No one knew what had happened to him, he just vanished off the face of the earth and then reappeared on my doorstep the night before he died, demanding your address."

"Which you gave him?" I asked.

"No."

"Oh," I said, digesting this slowly. "Well who did then?"

"Your mother."

"Mother!"

"She rang that night in a terrible state. She said she needed to speak to you, that Toby had been round and that we were all in for it as Toby had decided to come clean about what he'd done. I presumed at the time that she meant about being your biological father but when Mavis turned up with a letter Toby had left for her, we decided to get hold of you first."

"So what happened?"

"By the time we'd tracked you down Toby was dead and you were being escorted to the nearest hospital, under armed guard."

"Ah."

"It was Mavis who suggested getting you out and had a plan. We just supplied a few things."

"Like what?"

"The doll and the wig were props for my friend Lionel's next show. He's a magician for adult men-only clubs," Ben said.

I tried to work out just exactly what a magician could possibly do with a life-size blow-up doll with fully inflatable genitalia and after coming to the conclusion he could do practically anything he wanted, I lifted my mind out of the sewer and asked, "And the drugs, where did they come from?"

"I have my sources," Mavis smugly replied.

"I bet you do!" I snapped.

"I got you out, you ungrateful little brat! Have you any idea what they would have done to you?" she shouted, standing up and throwing the cushion at me.

"No, but I expect you're going to tell me," I shouted back, red in the face and for some reason really angry now. What right had she got to save me anyway and what had my family problems got to do with her?

"Sit down, both of you," my father growled, fixing us both with his polar bear stare. You might think polar bears are large fluffy white things – I used to. However, after I had been on a so-called educational trip to the far north with Clarris and the rest of the entourage, I had come to the conclusion that the last thing you ever wanted to be cuddled by was a polar bear, especially a hungry one. The huge bus-like truck we were travelling in had broken down and three bears had started moving towards us, very fast. They nearly had the truck over before the rangers turned up and scared them off. I could see it in the bears' eyes, the same thought: "Great packed lunch!" And all they had to do was open the tin.

"Mavis has just as much right to be here as you. Mavis, show Edwin the letter." Mavis hesitated and then dragged a fold of mangled paper from her pocket and reluctantly handed it over. I gingerly unfolded the water-damaged page and squinted down at the badly scrawled handwriting.

Dear Mavis,

I have to find your brother Edwin, there are things he has to know.

Scotland didn't work, he's as mad as all the rest, madder if truth were told.

I think Warwick knows about the formula. I have to persuade him to go to the PM. What we have now could just about work.

I love you,

Dad.

"Brother – Dad ..." I spluttered.

"That's right, she's your sister and if you want to stay alive I'd start being a little nicer to her," my father admonished, patting me on the shoulder as he passed, the empty coffee jug cradled in his hands.

I sat in my stunned and stationary position and stared at Mavis, who stared back.

"So," I said, breaking the silence.

"Care to fill me in on Mr Warwick and why I caught him trying to inject me with this – whatever it is?" I asked, extracting a carefully wrapped newspaper package containing the hypodermic fragment I'd retrieved from under my hospital locker.

There was still a miniscule amount of liquid in the bottom, which I'd carefully wrapped in the clingfilm that had previously covered my sponge pudding, and a plastic urine screw top sample bottle I'd found in the bathroom.

"What is that stuff?" Mavis asked, peering at it.

"I have no idea," I replied. "Except that I had a sneaky feeling it wasn't to make me feel better."

Mavis and I looked at each other and grinned. Perhaps suddenly finding out that you had a sister wasn't all that bad.

chapter seven

MI7: The department that never was

Mavis and I sat back and considered our options. I could, I thought, take the first boat to Europe and disappear or I could stay and try and find out what it was that had got my newly acquired father killed. After all, Mavis was still one of the toughest nuts in the media tree, so snooping, sabotage, bribery and corruption would all be just another day's work.

Having made up my mind I set about persuading Mavis to break the ingrained habit of a lifetime and tell me the truth, the whole truth and nothing but the truth.

"Who is Mr Warwick?" I asked.

"A member of MI7."

"Who?"

"Not who, what." Mavis sucked in her cheeks and scratched the lobe of her left ear thoughtfully. "During the days before the New Management."

"When men were top of the dung heap?"

"I see you've read your history books."

"Got a B+ cred.," I stated proudly.

"You mean apart from your natural attributes you can read and write?" Mavis grinned.

"Let's leave my private bits out of this, shall we?"

We both knew that I'd only managed to get onto the lower rung of the IT pool ladder before I'd been spotted in the communal shower at the local gym by one of Clarris Sharpe's aides. Impressed by both my youth and significant inches, I'd been offered the job of personal assistant to one of the brighter political stars. Clarris was in her late twenties when we had met and still had that raw sexual charisma that many women in positions of increasing power seemed to have. The flat she showed me round in Canary Wharf was huge in comparison to my own and the other guys, Mark and Pete were OK. So I took the job. Mother had a fit and called me all the names under the sun. Dad hadn't been exactly overjoyed. But the money was good; I got six weeks' paid holiday a year and all the usual advantages of a government position. I was also hounded by the press for any dirt on my mistress and had to put up with the usual barbed and derisory comments from the other guys I'd grown up with, who still had to work for a living.

And what did I do to earn my embarrassingly large salary? I had to provide sexual fulfilment day or night, in any position and under any circumstance to my lady employer, and some I had to admit were pretty unusual. I also had to help keep the flat clean, provide a warm and happy environment and listen to my mistress without blabbing anything to anybody else – or more importantly and much more difficult – not to show how mind-numbingly boring it all was. To be honest, without the safety valve of being able to talk it over with my flatmates I'd probably have gone a little insane. They were my surrogate family, especially Pete. Although since he'd injured his back and had had to be invalided out things had not been quite the same.

Now Clarris was Minister for Home Affairs and was a very powerful lady indeed; some said she was next in line for the job of President. I wasn't so sure she'd accept but just at this present moment I'd have given almost anything to have been snuggled up on a big fake fur rug with a bottle of Bollinger and Clarris Sharpe's brain at my disposal. The body wasn't bad either and I bet Mavis would have given a month's salary to know what she could do with a roll of clingfilm, tub of chocolate spread and a punnet of fresh strawberries.

"What are you grinning at?" Mavis asked sharply, bringing me back to reality with a bump.

"Nothing," I said, trying for the hurt and innocent look.

"Why have you gone red?" she asked.

"Er ... you were going to tell me about MI7," I said, hastily changing the subject.

Mavis gave me a suspicious 'what are you up to' look but continued anyway. "Oh yes. Well, before the riots there was a certain amount of spying and general nefarious goings on. Terrorism etc."

"MI5 and MI6," I agreed, nodding. "It was in my book on political history in Year 12," I added, trying to be helpful.

"So you'll remember that under the New Management they were disbanded."

"Surplus to requirements," I agreed, quoting the official line.

"Except that they still exist under the title MI7 and under

the direct control of the Attorney General."

"Not the President?" I asked, shocked.

"No."

"Oh."

"So why are you so certain that your Mr Warwick was trying to harm you?" Mavis asked, folding her fingers together in a sort of bridge, over the top of which she rested a sharp, lightly tanned chin.

"I don't know. Thing is, at the beginning of last week I had to deliver some papers to Clarris at the House."

"Westminster?"

"Yes. She'd left them behind after she'd …" My voice tailed off as I remembered. Mentally giving myself a cuff around the ears I continued. "Well anyway, she rang to say she needed them and me immediately. So I got a taxi and went up to her office. Well, as I was creeping round one of the back stairways I spotted this Warwick character coming out of the Speaker's office. He was acting a bit shifty, if you know what I mean; he kept looking around and then when he thought no one was about, he turned and wiped the doorhandle with a large handkerchief and scuttled off."

"And where were you?"

"I'd hidden behind one of the pillars on the corner; it's not that well lit and it's one of the known camera blind spots."

"How do you know that?" Mavis asked, her journalist's nose twitching.

"Oh, you just know," I said vaguely, as if I spent a lot of time delivering notes. The truth was that Clarris had demanded my services one evening, because for once the House was sitting late; normally they stopped at 5.30 and cleared off up to the Members' Bar. She said she wanted to clear her mind, which meant she wanted me to take her up against the corner pillar wearing nothing but a long leather trenchcoat. Actually it had been fun, if a little nervewracking as the coat kept slipping down against the marble and it made standing up and providing my usual exemplary gymnastics extremely difficult. Which is how I came to know about that particular blind spot. There were others, most of which I've discovered over the three years of my employment. There was a particular cleaning cupboard, which had this ledge halfway up ... I could feel a slight stirring in the works department so with a jolt forced my mind back to the present and reaffixed my gaze upon Mavis, whilst at the same time placing a tapestry-clad cushion over my lap.

"So he wiped the doorhandle?" Mavis said, thoughtfully staring down at her feet.

"Looked like it," I agreed.

"What do you reckon he was doing there?"

"I have no idea but I did think it was a little odd that the Speaker was taken seriously ill three hours later."

"Good grief, so she was." Mavis looked up from the floor, a stunned expression on her face. Ideas were beginning to form in that steel trap of a brain; I could almost see the cogs moving

"Coincidence?"

"With the Warwick involved, I doubt it very much."

"But why?"

"What was she working on at the time, do you know?"

"Not really. There was talk of a new committee she was chairing that had something to do with meetings over the Scottish border sanctions."

"Scotland?"

"Yeah, pretty grim, huh? Imagine living in there. I mean it's still run by the old guard. Bet you anything you like that the trains are late and nothing works."

"That's where Toby went."

"What!"

"The year he disappeared he went to Scotland. Well, I think he did. I managed to track him down to the Newcastle Brown checkpoint and then he simply ceased to exist."

"What did your Mum think about it all?" I asked tentatively – after all, apart from the fact that we'd shared the same sperm, so to speak, I knew nothing more about her.

"Mother said good riddance to bad rubbish and went back to work."

"Your mother, is she the one that owns the Skoda?" I'd been dying to ask as the only people who were allowed to have their own cars were teachers, medical staff and the police and emergency services. Journalists took the bus or the train like everyone else. My mother had a car, as she was now head of the local primary school and I was intrigued to find out what Mavis's mother did. Perhaps she too taught monsters for a living and had the heady delight of applying a metre rule to their flabby behinds when they misbehaved. Mother said it was a major highlight of the job. I hoped she was kidding, although remembering my own youth and the liberal application of the gym shoe I had my doubts.

"Yes, she works in the hospital."

"The one I was in."

"Yes."

"Oh."

"Actually, you met her." Mavis added, her eyes glinting with suppressed laughter.

"Oh?"

"Matron."

"Not the blue avenger!" I spluttered.

"One and the same; in fact she said you reminded her very strongly of our mutual recently deceased ancestor."

"Oh yes?"

"Yes." Mavis looked at me a thoughtful expression on her face. "She said she'd have recognized your er … attributes anywhere, in fact she said it was the only thing he was ever any good at."

"How did she …?" My voice tailed off as I remembered that somebody had kindly left my underwear in my locker and I certainly hadn't been in a fit state to do anything, let alone undress.

"Exactly." Mavis chuckled nastily. I was really going to have to buy that mask.

"So she knew about the escape bid?"

"Sort of. Well she said she didn't want to know but she told me I had twelve hours tops and lent me the car. She also left a hypo of anaesthetic lying on my trolley when I went round with the lunches. I'm quite public-spirited really; community service every week." I looked at her in open disbelief. Until, that is, she added, "You'd be surprised how much gossip you can get hold of in the A&E department on a busy Saturday night."

I grinned back at her. I could well imagine what sort of dirt she could dig up, especially in the wee small hours when the private clubs and casinos disgorged their well-heeled members. Well, that at least explained why Matron hadn't noticed the doll under the bed. And why she'd been so keen to have Mr Warwick thrown out.

"Won't she get into trouble?" I asked.

"Mum!" Mavis laughed outright. "Do you honestly think anyone would be brave enough to even suspect her, let alone ask her?"

"No," I agreed ruefully. "So what do we do now?"

"We get you out of London, as far away from the department and the police as possible and retrace our reprehensible father's steps all the way to Scotland if necessary."

"*Scotland* – but nobody ever goes there!"

"Oh yes they do," Mavis muttered, getting up and stretching, cat-like. "They just never come back."

chapter eight

The *Maybole Rose*

Bill and Ben were sitting in the kitchen sharing a fat, sweet-smelling joint and listening to Radio 2, when we emerged from the lounge. Mavis stood in the doorway and surveyed them with what I can only describe as a fond expression, or about as fond as sharks get when they're off duty.

"Right you two, we have work to do," she remarked in a businesslike fashion.

"Edwin and I need a complete makeover and we need enough provisions for about a week. Not too heavy, and some spare clothes." I gaped at her; why not ask for a get-away car and a couple of weapons while we're at it as well, I thought.

Dad – after all whatever biology might say to the contrary you can't just wipe out twenty-three years of knee plastering, hugs, bedtime stories and being yelled at a lot – didn't seem at all perturbed. He just looked at us for a few long hard minutes and then, smiling, beckoned Mavis and I to a small staircase, which went up to the attic.

"'Come into my parlour', said the spider to the fly," he

quoted, sounding so much like an old Vincent Price movie that I got tiny goosebumps down my spine.

The room we entered was so full of light I had to blink several times to clear my vision. The room was long and narrow and was lit by three large dormer windows on one side and two skylights on the other. There were chairs set around the edge, a long table covered in jars and brushes, bits of cloth and what looked like a couple of plastic ears and a large nose. One of the chairs was positioned in front of the kind of sink you'd find in any local hairdressers and looked to my experienced eye just about as uncomfortable.

"I think," my father muttered, "that what we need to do is to find a new personality and then fit the image to match. Mavis, for you we will remove the sophisticated about-town girl and change her into Little Miss Mouse and you, Edwin, need to have fallen on hard times." I narrowed my eyes and glared at him – hard times? How much further did I have to fall!

Chuckling, he made Mavis sit on one of the chairs while he applied some sort of evil smelling goo to the roots of her hair. Then it was my turn. After a while he put some more on and finally satisfied, washed it out. It was during the massaging out of the shampoo and massaging in of the conditioner that I fell asleep.

I came to with a start as a woman with closely cropped, light mousy, almost grey hair, glasses, scruffy top, trousers and threadbare trainers began to knead the back of my neck. It took me a while to realize it was Mavis grinning back at me from the mirror, which had been carefully angled in front of my face.

"Mavis?" I queried, taking in the new look.

"Do you like?" she asked, pirouetting on the spot.

"Um …" I stalled for time. "You look interesting."

"Edwin, it's your turn now," said my father, beckoning me to the chair placed carefully in the centre of the room. He had a pair of evil-looking scissors in one hand and what looked suspiciously like a staple gun in the other.

With a certain degree of trepidation I sat.

"Close your eyes," he said in his commanding voice. "And don't open them again until I've finished."

When I did open them again it was because of the sudden pain in my left ear.

"There!" said my father, positively crowing with pride in his handiwork. "Take a look, young Kyle."

"Kyle!" I looked into the mirror held in front of me and gasped as Kyle stared back. Gone were the carefully groomed glossy chestnut curls and clean-cut good looks. In their place was a black spiky-haired lout with terrible skin and not one but two gold hoops and a stud in his left ear. A pair of wire-framed glasses were handed to me and what with that and the unshaved stubble on my chin my fond parent had actually made me look like someone who'd very recently escaped from some form of government institution.

"You too look …" observed Mavis, "interesting."

"You should try and keep the stubble and cultivate a moustache of some sort. When the dye begins to grow out you can always add some axle grease – it'll look about the same colour or near enough when wet."

My father walked around me surveying his handiwork and then as if satisfied dumped a pile of clean but tatty clothes at me. I sighed; there didn't appear to be a designer label in any of them.

Finally I emerged from the curtained off cubicle in the corner and bowed to a stunned and delighted audience.

With my new baggy jeans, checked shirt and scruffy black leather boots I looked like a trainee car mechanic with several years of hot-wiring experience behind him. Mavis had to hold on to Ben who'd emerged from the kitchen downstairs to view my transformation.

"Well," he said, pursing his lips in a deliberately camp way. "If I ever fancy a bit of rough I know who to call."

"Great," I muttered, grinning sheepishly.

It had suddenly dawned on me that what my Father actually did wasn't just movie makeup but the invention of personalities, because I actually felt different, in fact very much like a Kyle or at least the ones I'd met.

"Well, much as we'd like you to stay for lunch we really feel that in the circumstances it might be better if you left," Ben stated, handing us a heavy rucksack each. I put mine on and adjusted the harnesses so that it at least felt a little more comfortable.

With a hug from my father and a promise to be good and take care, we were escorted back down to the garage where a van waited, its doors open at the side. Ben ushered us into the back and then began to carefully pile trays of baking in front of us, until we were entirely hidden.

Then the garage doors were opened. I had noticed that the Skoda had gone, so presumed someone had driven it back to the hospital either during the early hours or while I'd been undergoing my metamorphosis backwards from a butterfly to a grub.

More baskets and trays were loaded. I hoped that anybody watching would just assume it was the normal delivery. After what seemed like hours the doors were shut and bolted and the van rattled out of the garage, paused while the garage was closed behind us and then trundled off down the lane at the back of the house. Mavis and I bounced and bobbed with the laden trays as the van picked up speed. I presumed we had hit the motorway, which I'd seen from the windows of my father's rooftop eyrie. Finally the van slowed and after about twenty minutes of turns and bumps it stopped.

The van doors swung open, letting in a grey heavy light and a damp drain smell. We were in some sort of basement. Carefully the trays and baskets were carried away into the darkness, until eventually we had room to edge around the remainder and stumble from the van.

"Quick," Ben muttered, looking around. "The porter will be back in a minute. You see that side door?" He pointed at a green roughly painted door in the wall and we nodded. "Go through there along the back alley and out by the side gate. If you then cut across the embankment and go about a mile or two cross-country through the woods you'll come out at the *Maybole Rose*. Good luck," he added hastily.

"Thanks," we said in unison, and suddenly realizing that maybe he wasn't such a big bad wolf, I turned back and gave him a brief hug and a second muffled thanks. Ben froze, taken completely off guard but as we opened the door in the wall and I briefly stole a glimpse back, I saw him wipe his eyes with his sleeve and after blowing his nose loudly move round to the front of the van.

Mavis and I followed Ben's instructions to the letter. We took great care to keep our heads down as we quickly navigated the alley and the embankment behind. As we walked towards the woods we could hear a fast train, hidden from view, rattle towards us and then away, its horn blaring at some unseen signal box.

The woods were cool and shade-dappled, the leaves

giving off a clean earthy smell underfoot. Somewhere in the gold-edged depths a stream gurgled and tumbled. After about an hour of brisk walking we emerged at the side of a long, straight stretch of water. Bright green duckweed marbled its surface and insects darted and skittered in front of us. Along the grass and reed fringed edges ducks and moorhen bobbed and dived, between the land and the water, their cries the only sound in the sun-stilled air.

"Where is this?" I asked.

"A branch of the old canal that joins up eventually with the Thames," Mavis informed me, shrugging her heavy load into a more comfortable position. Then with a nod to me to follow, she began to walk along the towpath away from the woods into a field-rimmed picture postcard of sun, sky and water. The canal twisted its way in front of us, small brick bridges looping and arching over its reflective surface.

It was very pretty and at any other time I'd have been more than happy to amble along but I was becoming increasingly worried. It was almost lunchtime, I was hungry, hot and sticky and I had absolutely no idea where we were going.

"Mavis?" I asked.

"Shush!" she admonished, waving me back into the shelter of a bridge we were passing under. Before us on the other side of the canal squatted a green and red brightly painted barge, its small round windows protecting the interior with thick heavy nets.

After carefully inspecting the surrounding area, Mavis, her nose and ears twitching with the concentration and air of a beagle, moved back around the side of the bridge, crossed it and quietly approached the barge. She took a key from her jacket pocket and after clambering on board opened the heavily varnished doors leading to the interior. Satisfied that all was in order she gave me the thumbs-up sign. I scuttled from under the bridge; across the top and down the other side very much like a displaced hermit crab who had temporarily lost its shell. Breathing heavily, I jumped across the narrow divide between bank and boat and with a feeling of relief dived down into the depths of the boat.

Mavis closed the door behind us and took off her rucksack. The inside of the barge was like the interior of a wooden box lined with dark red velvet. Everything was small, compact and smelt of lavender. It was quite possibly the most beautiful space I'd ever been in.

"Welcome," Mavis declared, "to the *Maybole Rose*."

chapter nine

Getting to know you

The *Maybole* was about forty-two foot long from stem to stern and appeared to be a lot bigger from the inside than when viewed from the side of the canal.

"Well, what do you think?" Mavis asked, watching me.

"You sure this shouldn't be called the 'Maybole Tardis?'" I replied as I opened a small cupboard under the sink and discovered enough tins to keep a hungry army on the march for a week.

Up at the front there was a dark, heavily varnished dining table, held up by two squat metal poles. A red velvet-covered L-shaped bench seat ran along the side of the boat up to a small kitchen area. A television perched on a corner cupboard and a plethora of cupboards and shelves were filled to the brim with everything you could possibly need, from charts and tatty paperbacks to an unopened bottle of twenty-year-old single malt.

The kitchen area had been compactly arranged next to the lounge/dining area with the left hand side of the boat free as an open corridor, which ran from one end of the barge to the other.

While I'd been gleefully exploring, Mavis had begun the task of unpacking our supplies from Ben. She'd deposited her haversack on the small varnished area between the stainless steel sink and the gas cooker and was now distributing the innards to various cupboards and drawers, one of which turned out to be an artfully disguised fridge.

Feeling like a kid at Christmas who'd been let loose in Toymaster, I turned and began to look around the other end of the boat. Next to the kitchen was a small shower and toilet with a washbasin suspended from the wall. Beyond this welcome token of civilization was a small wardrobe built into the side of the boat, next to two single beds, one on either side with their own view of water, leaves and flickering light.

There was even, to my delight, a radiator alongside each bed and it was warm. I couldn't quite believe my luck: this was a boat with central heating. Even the caravans I'd holidayed in as a child hadn't had that and as for a toilet and shower, I could still remember tumbling out of the metal-rimmed door of our cramped holiday home, in the early mist-strewn hours of the morning, for the municipal toilets, which in the cold dew-encrusted air had always managed to move at least half a mile further down and the water when you did get there was invariably either cold or 'off'. There was never any sign of a toilet roll and the dryers were always switched off with no visible means of turning them back on again.

Mavis suddenly materialized at my side and threw her rucksack on one of the two beds.

"I've emptied mine, now it's your turn. Come on, spill it out and let's see what goodies we have still to come."

She sat on the bed, which was covered with a dark blue candlewick bedspread, and watched me open my own backpack with unconcealed interest. Carefully I began to unearth various items; one torch with spare batteries taped to the rubber encased grip, a box of matches in a plastic bag, a large hunk of cheese, three packs of smoked bacon, ten packs of assorted dried products, all of which could be reconstituted with water to make mash, rice, couscous etc., a selection of fresh, carefully trimmed and prepared vegetables all vacuum packed for the freezer, toothpaste, toothbrush, a variety of squashed clothes including a week's supply of boxer shorts and in a ribbon- decorated foil-wrapped box, an economy pack of condoms with the legend 'novelty ends' written on the side in purple ink.

Mavis crowed with delight and after I had stowed my small amount of worldly goods under my bed in a little drawer, which also contained a motley collection of clean towels, packed with small silken lavender bags, I belatedly joined in the laughter, having finally seen the funny side.

"I suppose," Mavis said, wiping the tears from her eyes with the edge of her sleeve, "we'd better sort out something to eat and then work out a plan of attack."

"OK," I said, my stomach rumbling loudly in agreement, as we made our way back down to the galley.

Mavis ordered me to sit and handed over a can of lager and two glasses. While I was pouring she produced as if by magic two plates of chicken salad and a fresh baguette with a pack of butter.

"How did you do that?" I gaped, grabbing my plate and tearing off a chunk of the bread, which I lavishly spread with butter, my diet having gone out of the window with my hair and designer clothes.

"Ben stuck a small freezer bag in my sack – it contained a fair amount of fresh foods, including the salad," Mavis replied, her fork stabbing at a sliver of chicken and garlicky dressing.

After we'd finished and the kettle was on for coffee, Mavis sat back and sighed with stuffed contentment.

"I love this place," she remarked, stretching. "Now down to business."

I got up and moved towards the kitchen area and the happily hissing kettle.

"You, Edwin, are going to have to learn to pander to the engine and steer the boat. We also have to go through the cupboards and ensure we have everything. The engine provides the electricity, so as long as we are frugal at night and keep the engine running the rest of the day, then we'll be all right. Hot water for the shower, washing-up and central heating is provided by the gas boiler hidden in the cupboard between the kitchen and the bathroom and we have to fill the water tank at least once a day and sort out the soil tank once a week."

"Soil tank?" I asked.

"From the toilet. It's a bit temperamental, so to be on the safe side we pump it out and check the system once a week."

"Once a week? Just how long is this going to take us?" I asked.

"I don't know, a month maybe? Depends on the traffic and how fast you get at opening and closing locks."

"And can we really get all the way up to Scotland?"

"We can't go all the way in this. But we can reach the Midlands and from there I have a cunning plan for the rest." Mavis looked at me with something almost akin to vague affection, which was a welcome change from her previous one of undisguised contempt.

"The thing is we can't get out of London by car because we're not entitled to drive one and the police will be checking all vehicles just in case. Coaches and trains are out because of the county checks and we can't walk it. Apart from the fact I'm not used to cross country hikes we'd have to stay somewhere and we'd be noticed."

"Hence the barge," I said, getting up and walking to the open door leading onto the bow of the boat.

"That's right," Mavis agreed, joining me.

"Just how safe is it?" I asked.

"Well, we don't look like our old selves and a lot of people live on or around the canal system. We'll just look like a couple of travelling out-of-work youngsters, or better still we can always say we're students studying the canal system as a year out. All anyone will do is snigger into their beer at the thought of us doing the longest pub crawl ever and it being paid for by some government grant."

"Not a bad idea," I said, cradling my quickly cooling coffee. "Then all we do is stop for water, fuel and fresh supplies, blend in and disappear."

"Exactly."

A sudden thought occurred to me. "Is that what happened to Tobias?" I asked.

"Yes," Mavis agreed, staring beyond me to the fields on either side. Somewhere a dog barked.

"Was this his boat then?" I asked.

"No," she replied, turning her back on me.

"Oh."

"It was Mike's."

"Mike who?"

"Mike." There was a short pause before she continued: it was almost as if the infamous wordsmith had run out of suitable words. "My husband."

"Your what?" I knew I must have looked like a goldfish that had accidentally left the bowl because I felt my jaw drop and Mavis gave me that look.

"My husband," she repeated, moving back into the boat and down towards the door at the back. There was a distinctly frosty edge to the voice, which did not in any way encourage further questions, especially the ones I wanted to ask. Erring on the side of caution, I mentally buttoned my lip. There were an awful lot of pubs from here to Scotland and I could wait.

"You cast off the bow rope while I start the engine. Then get back here and let go of the stern." She turned at my lack of acknowledgement and expelled air in the manner of a resigned tortoise. "The bow is the front or pointy bit and the stern is the back or end. OK?"

I nodded and went outside. The rope stretched from a hook at the very front to a metal stake half buried in the canal bank. I leapt across the shifting water dividing the dry from the very wet and girded my loins.

After about five minutes and the application of brute force I had the spike out of the ground, cast the rope free and tossed it into the well of the barge. Mavis, who'd been watching my efforts across the barge roof, gave me a slow handclap which would have been insulting if it hadn't have been for the broad grin accompanying it.

I executed a short mocking bow and returned to her end of the boat where the stern rope was wrapped around a rusty-looking metal ring, attached to a slab of grey concrete, set into the bank.

The rope had moved, dried and soaked over a period of time and was harder to release than the other. In the end I pushed the metal spike into a small pocket of space and alternatively pushed and pulled it away from itself. Finally it moved and I managed to release the *Maybole Rose* from her mooring. Covered in sweat, I looked up and holding onto the end of the rope, waited for Mavis to tell me what to do.

The engine throbbed and put-putted, eager to be away, and finally satisfied, Mavis gave me the thumbs up and called, "Right then, cast off."

I threw the rope into the back of the boat, narrowly missing her feet and stood like a lemon on the shore.

Mavis gave me a superior look and asked with her old sarcasm. "Are you going to just stand there or jump back on, because I'm going?"

'Idiot,' I muttered under my breath and jumped back on board. The boat had by then moved away from the bank and it was only as I soared into the air that I wondered how deep the canal actually was. For a brief adrenalin-prickling moment I honestly thought I was going to miss, but Mavis, who'd deserted the tiller, grabbed me as I stumbled and set me right side up beside the lifebelt, attached to a metal balustrade at the back.

We were off on the great adventure.

I wasn't sure how it would turn out.

All I did know was that suddenly from being the only child of two parents who'd stopped communicating I had over the space of twenty-four hours acquired an extra Dad, a sister and it appeared an in-law. With any luck I'd have the full quota of aunts, uncles and assorted kissing cousins by the time we got to the very north. Or I mused, folding

the rope into a neat ring rather like a curled cobra, I'd be dead.

chapter ten

A cunning plan!

We hadn't gone very far down our narrow winding canal before we passed under an old wrought iron-rimmed bridge and simultaneously hit civilization and the Thames. It was like hitting the rush hour on the M25, only marginally wetter. There were boats and barges everywhere and they all appeared to know what they were doing.

Mavis had been attempting to initiate me into the dark art of steering, with little if any success. You think it's a piece of cake, nothing to it, that is until you take what they call the tiller, which is basically a long bit of painted metal with a handle at the end. Then you realize that you can steer away like mad and nothing happens. Mavis said I had to learn to think in advance and turn the boat before anything cropped up like bends, bridges and other boats. I did try, and after I hit my third bank and second bridge I was almost getting the hang of it. It was a bit like bumper cars with water only an awful lot bigger. The other thing I had to learn was how to control the engine. After a while I realized it was just like the shower in the flat – it hated me. I also became painfully aware that, after the third bargee had threatened me with termination and the insertion of a boathook with I might add extreme prejudice, the *Maybole Rose* was female and as such was going to take no bloody notice of me at all. Eventually, Mavis, on seeing my look of abject terror as I narrowly missed two boats, a coal barge and a family of ducks, firmly retook the helm and pointed me in the direction of the galley.

Later, as I watched the world on the other side of the green, carefully manicured lawns of the riverbank slip by at the racy speed of three miles per hour, I asked the thought uppermost in my mind.

"Mavis?"

"Um."

"Aren't we going the wrong way?"

"What do you mean?"

I pointed at the far side where unmistakably expensive houses were wandering into view and a few, tall, well-known landmarks could be seen hovering in the background.

"I thought we were getting away from London?"

"We are."

"Right."

"It's part of my cunning plan."

"Good."

"What we do is we make our way north slowly."

I nodded, watching a small black moorhen race past the bow without so much as a backward glance; the wretched bird must have been going at least twice as fast as we were.

"But first," Mavis coughed nervously, "we have to go back through London to Teddington, turn left at Kew and get onto the canal to Cowley. From there we travel up to Watford and stay on the Grand Union until we get to the

Norton Junction."

"Then what?" I asked, trying to work out where the hell Norton was. Frankly I was beginning to wonder if she was making this up. I was, after all, one of those people who believed that if it wasn't on the junction of a motorway it didn't exist.

"Don't you worry about it, brother dear." Mavis must have been reading my mind because she thrust a plastic-covered chart at me and shooed me back into the confines of the boat.

"Read that. And don't come back out until it's dark and we're safely moored. I don't want anyone recognizing you and blowing my chance of an exclusive!" She laughed at the panicked look on my face and in a slightly kinder tone continued her monologue. "This bit of the Thames is always chocker and I can usually find someone to help with the locks. We'll moor up at the first space after the tidal locks at Teddington and I'll treat you to one of my toasted tripledecker bacon and egg specials."

"Oh good, I can't wait," I muttered, curling up on my gently rocking bed. I did try to focus on the map in my hand but within two or three minutes was snoring gently as the *Maybole Rose* chugged along towards the grand metropolis of London and my old and very dead previous life.

chapter eleven

Teddington Lock and the fish slappers

It was dark when I woke up, apart from the strained yellow light which was decorating the surface of my bed with whirls of shifting colour. Outside, a streetlamp valiantly defied the encroaching night and I could hear the gentle and dulcet tones of an approaching boatman. That is, I could hear a lot of swearing accompanied by the sound of an engine which obviously needed the last rites. There was a brief moment of silence before the simultaneous explosion of metal hitting metal and a northern accent muttering, "Oh shite, that's fucked it all right. Proper pig's breakfast."

I sat up from the floor onto which I'd been tipped and rubbed the sore bits I could reach. I could hear Mavis remonstrating in true journalistic fashion, the language very blue and as far as I could judge fairly accurate, anatomically speaking. Blinking, owl-like in the sudden glare of dockside civilization I jumped ship and tottered off towards the noise of battle.

Mavis stood on the foredeck, a large silver-coloured winch in one hand and a frying pan in the other. My stomach, with a sudden surge of digestive juices, remembered the magic words 'egg and bacon tripledecker' and I prayed fervently to whoever was on duty in the great cock-up in the sky, that she hadn't started cooking.

"You great steaming git!" Mavis shouted. "I've got bits of bacon and partially cooked eggs all over the bloody floor."

"Thanks a bunch," I muttered, glaring skywards.

"It's all right love, I'll clean it up," the voice from across the water promised.

"Too f'ing right you will," Mavis replied, the frying pan glinting in the reflected light.

"Oi you there, hold this while I tie this stupid sodding bitch up," the voice demanded. I must have looked a bit stunned because it hastily added. "No, not her, you pillock – the boat."

I jumped back in time for a large coil of rope to wetly miss most of me and then ran forward, as it began to snake back into the water. Catching it in both hands I began to pull the elderly rusting hulk towards the bank.

There was a grunt of thanks as our attacker emerged from the gloom equipped with a couple of metal tow spikes and one of the largest mallets I'd ever seen.

"Thanks lad," he growled as he passed.

Mavis, still swearing in the time-honoured fashion of most fishwives, helped guide the rusting barge to its berth and then watched in helpless fascination as our new neighbour went about the business of securing the incredible rusting hulk for the night. Finally, after much tugging, pulling and cajoling, the thing was done and in a slightly more conciliatory voice our attacker asked for permission to come aboard. Mavis, now armed with a bucket of detergent and a large mop, agreed. Thrusting the implements at him she pointed wordlessly at the galley floor and handed me a can of beer.

"I could do with one of them, if you've spare, lass?"

The floor had been sloshed and scoured in record time and the food debris miraculously cleared. Mavis stared at the floor and silently handed over the last can in the pack of four, a ring of plastic still attached to the top.

"The name's Murdock," Murdock stated, holding out a hand the size of a small dinner plate. We both shook the massive paw in a fairly solemn fashion while we took stock of each other.

Murdock was big. Everywhere. Most of it was muscle or had been in his youth. I would have put him at the shady side of forty, maybe early fifties. He had that quiet look that all very big men have, perhaps because they know that no one in their right mind would pick a fight with them. No one, that is, except Mavis.

"Sorry about that, love," Murdock stated, waving his arms around like the sails of a slowly rotating windmill. "Let me buy you a proper dinner to make amends like?" He gave a solemn lopsided smile reminiscent of a large St Bernard who'd already started on the brandy barrel.

"Well," Mavis said, uncertainly looking from me to our large companion.

"Won't take no for an answer, me," Murdock said in what I would call a firm voice. Put it this way, we could have said no but from the set expression of the grey eyes to the pursed narrowness of rubber lips, I'd have laid ready money on his tucking both of us under an arm and carrying us off anyway.

I've always been a bit of a reader and frankly if you'd managed to have crossed J. K. Rowling's Reubus Hagrid with Reginald Hill's Andy Dalziel you'd have come very close to 'our' Murdock.

"Er, thanks," I replied, avoiding eye contact with Mavis, as I added, "I'll get my coat. Mavis, do you want me to lock up?"

"I can do it," Mavis said, glaring back at me.

As I waited for Mavis to secure the *Maybole Rose*, I looked across to our neighbour's elderly vessel. It was an odd blue colour, which may have been bottle- green in a previous life. There were dents and scrapes along the side and it was called 'The Leaky Pig'.

"Interesting name," I said, to break the silence between Murdock and myself.

"Named after the wife."

I raised an eyebrow or two.

"She was originally called the 'Alicia Belle' up to the divorce," Murdock added, kicking a discarded can into the murky water surrounding his craft.

"So where are we off to?" Mavis asked, emerging from the shadows.

"The Fisherman's," Murdock replied, marching off along the concrete canal path.

"Fisherman's What?" Mavis asked.

"Dunno, that bit of the sign fell off and no one can remember what it was before. So it's just the Fisherman's. They do a bloody good steak and kidney, mind."

"Good, that's all I needed to know," Mavis muttered as both of us struggled to keep up.

The Fisherman's was an old brick square building, squatting in what looked like the municipal home of res for old cars. Yellow light and the sound of laughter were escaping from every window and doorway. Wafts of food-scented air assailed our nostrils as we drew within spitting distance. With Mavis pushed to the front we entered the low-slung doorway, the ceiling beyond dipping and bowing beneath the weight of the rooms above. Our collective salivary glands began to work faster than any of Pavlov's dogs as we inhaled the pungent aroma of garlic, herbs and glorious gravy.

Inside, Murdock somehow managed to acquire a table, and waving at the barman across the sea of heads, arms and shifting jumpers, demanded three pints of Peculiar and three Snake and Pidley puddings.

"Er … Snake and Pidley?" I asked.

"Aye, that's what it's called." I could tell he was about to enlarge on the subject when a hairy fist hammered into his back and a short wiry man with the face of a ferret joined us.

"Harold, me old mucker, you made it!" Murdock shouted gleefully as four pints mysteriously appeared on the table together with four sets of knives and forks, each wrapped in white paper napkins embellished with a large fish.

"You having the Rat Pie?" Harold asked, tucking one of the napkins under his chin.

"No, the Snake and Pidley. You?"

"Rat Pie for me, as always. Mind you, I've got to remember to leave a bit of room for the larks' vomit chocolate trifle," Harold added, taking a swig of beer. "Ah … nectar of the gods, positive ambrosia." He sighed, wiping his chin with the back of his hand.

I was about to say something on the grounds of what the hell sort of pub is this, when an old lady wearing leathers and a full set of whiskers entered the crowded room. She was accompanied by a tall thin man in a suit and a bowler hat who was carrying nonchalantly over one pinstriped shoulder, a three-foot-long inflatable foot.

Mavis and I blinked in astonishment and simultaneously took large gulps of beer. After the food had arrived together with four more pints we began to get into the swing of things. Harold and Murdock seemed to know everyone, including a man in a long fawn-coloured raincoat who had a blue parrot strapped to his shoulder. Every time anyone passed him they shouted things like, 'It's dead – if it hadn't been nailed to the perch ...' 'Pushing up the daisies ...' 'Gone to the great aviary in the sky ...' to which he always replied, 'It's not dead, it's just having a rest.'

After the pudding had been and gone, a sort of chocolate steamed sponge with sticky bits, and a few more pints had been consumed, Mavis and I wouldn't have been surprised to see an elephant dance on the table wearing a pink tutu and playing the euphonium, badly. That didn't happen but something else did.

At eleven O'clock exactly a gong sounded and the whole place stopped. Silently the pub was abandoned and we all congregated outside in the fashion of a particularly well-orchestrated and very quiet fire drill.

"What happens now?" Mavis asked, trying not to giggle.

"Shut up, you two," Murdock admonished, with a large podgy finger placed pointedly at his lips.

After a few minutes of shuffling and coughing two men emerged from the yellow light of the Fisherman's and followed by the entire clientele, marched in a military fashion back down towards the water and the topmost lock gate. The leaders were both dressed in khaki army-style shorts and military tops and both of them were holding dead fish.

When we got to the lock a whistle was blown and everyone crowded around for a good look. Those at the front knelt or squatted on their haunches with the biggest folk at the back.

Then the most extraordinary thing happened. The younger man, without the cap, did a sort of capering dance and slapped the taller, older chap in the face with his fish, and he didn't do it just once he did it over and over again and to music. Finally after about ten minutes of such violent laughter that most of the audience were threatening to lose total control of their bowels, he stopped, stood back and saluted his companion, who produced from nowhere that I could see, the largest fish outside a remake of *Jaws* and hit him full on the side of the head. There was a brief moment of silence before the dull splash as the first chap hit the water and then the entire lockside erupted into a roar of approval.

"Best fish-slapping dance ever," said the lady in oversized charwoman's overalls who was crouched down next to me.

"Oh," said Mavis, the light of knowledge dawning in her wet, laughter- rimmed eyes. "I should have guessed. Teddington Lock!"

"What?" I queried.

"Wait here," she demanded.

We stood to one side, as the crowd passed on its way back to the pub. When they had gone she pointed at a plaque screwed into the brick wall of the lockkeeper's house.

It read, '*In fond memory of proper television*', and underneath was a notice stating, 'The above plaque has been donated by the Monty Python Appreciation Society and is placed at the site of the annual re-enactment of the famous

Fish Slappers' Dance.'

chapter twelve

The morning after

I awoke curled up around a bright yellow plastic bucket and an elderly orange life preserver. My head throbbed, sending shafts of white dots into my eyes. For a moment I felt almost as if I could stand and then everything connected. Moments later I was crouched over the gunnels, sweat pouring down my face. I'd just about emptied most of my alimentary canal when Murdock brushed by me, clutching a mug of coffee and a bacon bap.

"Better out than in," he chuckled, giving me a playful slap on the shoulder in passing.

"It was the beer," I muttered, wiping my chin with the sleeve of my jumper. "There was something in it."

"Alcohol," Mavis uttered with all the unconcern and callousness of the hardy drinker.

It was as I was straightening up that I noticed something was wrong. Murdock had dropped his mug of coffee and was incoherently gurgling.

"Where the hell is my boat?" he bleated. "Some bugger's nicked it!"

Mavis rushed to stand by his side and stared out over the mist-wreathed river.

My head still completely full of razor blades, I looked down and there it was.

"Er Murdock," I said in carefully neutral tones, "I don't think anyone's pinched it or at least no one without a full set of diving gear."

"What?"

Murdock and Mavis followed my shakily pointing finger and there was an audible intake of collective breath.

"Bloody Nora!" Murdock intoned. "I thought I'd sorted out the valves on that bleedin' toilet."

We all stood and stared at the waterlogged remains of the Leaky Pig which glinted back at us from its watery grave. Something slithered from the open hatchway and rose to the surface; there was a glint of silver, a surge of bubbles and it dived back down to its new and palatial abode.

"Look at that!" Murdock roared. "I've not been gone five minutes and I've got bloody squatters."

Mavis tried to mutter something vaguely soothing but it was no good. Murdock slid to the deck and railed at great length and with Shakespearian emphasis against the fates and all their little helpers. As he continued, the language getting bluer by the minute, I couldn't help but see his point. Everything he'd owned had gone; his clothes, money, worldly comforts and more importantly his only mode of transport.

Mavis patted his arm in an absentminded fashion and handed him a fresh mug of coffee.

"Sorry about the language, love, I'm a bit upset," Murdock stated, wiping a stray drop of moisture away from the bags under his eyes.

"It's all right, I've heard a lot worse."

"Especially near the odd deadline, eh lass?"

There was a distinct and sudden frost as Mavis turned and faced him. Murdock stood his ground unflinching and I curled back down onto the deck, clutching the yellow bucket to me. Nobody spoke but there was a lot of eyebrow and chin adjustment going on.

"How did you know?" I asked, incurring the instant wrath of Mavis who tried to kick me but missed and got the bucket instead. Murdock gave a sudden grin and the temperature rose a few degrees.

"Would you believe it was a lucky guess?" Murdock asked, sinking down onto one of the side seats.

"No," was the brusque reply, as Mavis sat and scowled darkly back at him, from her perch on the bench opposite.

"Ah." Murdock stroked the stubble on his chin and gave her a speculative look. "Well, it was a combination of things really."

"Oh?"

"Of course if I tell you you'll have to kill me." Murdock grinned like a well-fed shark and Mavis sat and stared at him as if she'd like nothing better. Well, we all know what happened to Jaws. And as long as Mavis was unable to get her hands on an industrial chainsaw with a very long lead we were fairly safe from the re-enactment of the middle section of *Jaws 5*. I hoped. Of course there was that bit with the fire extinguisher and the acetylene torch with the variable head adjustment.

Nervously I shuffled back further into the corner, which was, my brain hissed to my body, a really stupid thing to do as both of them then turned their attention to me.

"Still not feeling well?" Murdock asked kindly. "I'll get you a mad Murdock special, put some colour back in your cheeks."

"Hang on a minute – I haven't –" Mavis squawked "finished."

"That went well." I muttered, trying to stand. Bits of me had gone to sleep and didn't want to go back to work and the strobe lights were still there somewhere behind my eyeballs, waiting.

"Oh for God's sake," Mavis muttered, helping me to stand and then sit. The world around me wobbled and then began to settle, as Mavis not unkindly pushed me down onto Murdock's seat. She gave me a cursory look not unlike that of her mother viewing the average road accident victim and handed me back my bucket. I was just trying to adjust to the noise of the passing river when Murdock arrived back clutching a squat glass of something brown and glutinous. There was a whole egg in it and it was looking straight at me.

"There you go, lad. Kill or cure, eh?" I continued to stare at it in a semi-stunned fashion.

"Well if you won't take your medicine like a man, you'll have to do it like a child. Mavis, hold him steady." Mavis grabbed me firmly by the shoulders and Murdock with the experience of years forced the evil stuff down my open mouth, which I'd unfortunately been unable to close in time. It was quite possibly the most disgusting thing I'd ever had to eat with the possible exception of my mother's version of Mediterranean fish stew.

They both backed off quickly as literally foaming at the mouth I turned and threw up into the Thames. Part of me wished most sincerely for death while the little bit of me which was trying for the recovery position raised its sodden head and felt marginally better.

Mavis handed me a dry if not overly clean cotton tea towel and Murdock disappeared back into the bowels of the boat muttering something about coffee.

Some fifteen minutes later we all sat in comparative peace sipping very strong, very fresh coffee with the occasional nibble at something which resembled buttered cardboard. It was actually edible if you managed to loosen the charred edges first.

Mavis had obviously inherited the family gene of not being able to cook anything not out of a packet. I was beginning to think I'd had a narrow escape from the egg and bacon special. Perhaps somebody up there was looking after me after all.

"So," said Mavis between chews. "How did you know?"

"It was the eyes. That and a certain way you have of holding your head. Edwin there was a bit easier – I've spent ages looking at fuzzy videos of him and Clarris Sharpe."

My blood curdled and ran cold. Who the hell would spend hours looking at videos of me, and much more importantly, why would they even want to?

Mavis must have been thinking along the same lines because she glanced at me very briefly as she searched around for something sharp or heavy and very blunt.

"Don't worry, you two would have fooled most people. After all I've spent years studying people's bone structures and other distinguishing features."

"What! You're not a plastic surgeon or something?" snapped Mavis, her eyes suddenly spotting the small axe fixed to the side of the boat with a length of leather. It had a label saying 'For emergency use only' stuck to its handle.

"No, I'm a cartoonist for the 'Weekly Carp'."

Mavis stayed the hand reaching below her seat for the implement of delivery and scowled at him.

"Good God, you can't be!"

"By George, I think she's got it."

"You can't be, not Poodles!"

Murdock nodded his head and grinned fiendishly at us.

Poodles. This giant of a man was actually Poodles, the master of the vitriolic doodle. I've actually lost count of the number of times some scurrilous, not to say extremely rude scribble has caused the Sharpe brows to knit together in anger. Clarris and the rest of the House would quite happily have nailed Poodles to the wall, stuffed or otherwise. In fact, after the last one I'd seen, involving myself in a suitable outfit – I think it was some sort of rescue gear involving little more than a hat and a strategically placed leather belt, I'd quite happily have thrown caution to the wind and held the taxidermist's tools. Which, funnily enough, was what Clarris was sort of doing in Poodle's last offering.

My cup had finally run over. Not only was I sharing a boat with the poisonous penpusher of Paddington Park but the despicable Doodler of Dulwich! Could the day get any worse?

"I've loved your stuff for ever. Well ever since I've understood the words." Mavis jumped up from her seat and hugged him; she even kissed him on his stubbly cheek. Sickened, I sat there staring, mouth wide and loose with all the air of a codfish awaiting the chop.

"I gather this means I can stay?" Murdock asked, rubbing his cheek in a pensive fashion, whilst regarding Mavis as one would an unexploded and quite possibly unstable bomb.

"Yes, why not?"

"But …" I managed to gurgle.

"It's all right Edwin. The police are looking for you and possibly me as well but they won't be looking for a family group of Dad and two twenty-year-olds. It's a perfect combination." She grinned at me before continuing in her best wheedling voice. Murdock was still visibly grappling with the word 'Dad'. "Oh come on Edwin, think of it this way, Murdock's used to boats and we've a long way to go. He can help with the locks and the tying up."

They both stared at me, waiting for some sort of reaction.

"Can you cook?" I asked after a long thought-filled silence.

"Aye, what I can't do with a tin of stewing steak and the humble spud ain't worth knowing lad."

"OK," I agreed. "You can stay."

Mavis was, on balance, right. We could do with an extra hand because what I knew about boats you could write on the side of a postage stamp and still have room for Big Ben and the Premier's blue-rinsed profile. Murdock could cook and whilst I could just about boil, mash and bake Mavis obviously had difficulty with anything you didn't add to water with a teaspoon.

Ten minutes later we were off, ropes neatly curled and the contents of our floating home methodically stowed away. Even the galley was spotless. Life with Murdock would be fraught with perils and the liberal imbibing of alcohol but I had the feeling that anything taken under his wing would be protected not only by hands which could tear telephone directories in half but by a mind even more devious and twisted than Mavis's own.

And so it was with a slightly more optimistic heart that I watched the brown and green mottled water slip by as we chugged gently down the Thames towards Kew Gardens and 'The North'.

chapter thirteen

Left hand down a bit

According to our map it should have taken a mere five hours to get from our stop at Teddington to the junction at Cowley. That was according to the map. Even then as I looked at the distance to be covered I had reckoned I could have walked it quicker. Mavis and Murdock had clearly banked on arriving at our final stop for the day, a little place they knew just north of Watford, by the time the pubs were due to open.

Unfortunately they hadn't reckoned on running into the Growler and Evil Ted. I mean it all started well; we chugged happily along past the gardens at Kew after the negotiation of the ornate and rather fascinating half tide locks at Richmond. I had stood watching from the safety of the pedestrian bridge while Murdock and Mavis did all the hard work. They had readily agreed to my slothful attitude not out of kindness but from the certain knowledge that I was almost completely useless when sober and when suffering from a self-inflicted brain tumour I was not just totally useless but positively dangerous. Besides which, I was getting a bit sick of Murdock's continual references to the dormouse in Alice in Wonderland. He'd even drawn a cartoon of me retching head first into an overly embellished Georgian teapot.

Halfway along the tree-fringed and gloriously green gardens at Kew we'd taken a left hand turn and entered the somewhat narrower confines of the Grand Union Canal.

Lunch was spent slowly chewing on a corned beef sandwich and watching the toothsome twosome arguing over how quickly they could get through the average lock. It had taken just under four hours to travel from Kew to Bulls Bridge Junction and then another hour to get to the Cowley Junction; both fascinating parts of the world populated by small children throwing stuff in as they sat by the canalside, fishing rods clutched in squat grimy hands. The second time an empty can had hit the deck Murdock had hit the roof and thrown it back. He must have practiced a lot because the aim was spot on and I presume the wretched boy still bears the scar. After that we were followed by a small troop of interested urchins hell-bent on seeing whether he would do it again.

He did, several times, each hit being greeted with loud hand clapping and applause. It wasn't my idea of travelling incognito but by the time he'd reached double figures I was curled up on my bunk, oblivious to everything but the steamroller in my head.

They evicted me from my comfortably rancid pit just before lunch, muttering words of encouragement and extolling the twin life-giving properties of fresh air and exercise.

It was then that fate took a hand.

On the other hand fate could have knocked off for a quick trip to the nearest deli, leaving his assistant in charge, you know, the one with red suit, horns, tail and a warped and twisted sense of humour.

We must have just about reached the junction because there were boats everywhere and tourist board signs had sprung up along the towpaths declaring the heady delights of a vast selection of entertainments from boat trips to Victorian tearooms. A variety of vessels had begun to cluster ahead as we neared the Slough Arm and a lot of them had simply stopped. It looked like the old pictures I'd seen of tailbacks on the M6, now a thing of historical record as most people now travelled by public transport. (Perhaps I ought to explain? You see when the New Management had taken over the helm the old Minister for Transport had loudly and publicly declared that the railway network was not, as they had stated in their manifest, completely crap. The New Management gave a collective and caustic sigh and bundled him onto a train near Land's End and told him to get to John O'Groats by the following day. They gave him the one hundred and twenty quid he said it would cost and then drove in convoy up to the land of fiery malt and the happy haggis. Cheating was out of the question as several members of the press, two TV broadcasters and an assortment of amused commuters went with him. He finally arrived five and a half days later, four hundred and thirty two pound fifty poorer, an amount underlined in red in our school history books and looking like something the cat would drag in, drag straight back out and then bury. Since then the transport network had had a complete overhaul, mostly financed by funds confiscated from the private accounts of the members of the old government, the majority of which had either died fairly horribly or had run away leaving no forwarding address. The last remnants of the House of Windsor had also abandoned ship, leaving behind a bemused janitor and several rotund, bad tempered Corgis. No one had actually realised just how much money you could save by not having the Royals and the cash then raised by the prudent sale of their various and numerous fixed assets had been invested in schools and the almost non-existent health service.)

I put my thoughtful ponderings on hold and viewed the boat jam ahead with a jaundiced eye. This, I thought, would really put the mockers on the dynamic duo's calculations. It promised to be a fairly long delay, as it appeared that someone had managed to back into an almost brand new motor cruiser, whose owner looked like he was going to explode. Whether it would be before or after the successful skewering of the idiot on the jetski who had forced the other boat to back up in the first place, only time would tell.

Murdock had by now settled down after temporarily mooring our boat, to await our turn through the mangled remains of a small rowing boat, the jetski and the cruiser. The owner of the iron-clad and elderly barge which had done the original damage, floated on the still water and calmly lit an old, less than aromatic pipe. Murdock pointed out vessels of interest as they plodded past whilst enjoying a late lunch of three rounds of corned beef and half a jar of pickled onions. Squeezing the last drop of ginger beer from the can in his hand he absentmindedly threw it towards the bank.

There was a howl of protest from the long malodorous grass verge and something small, round and clothed in what could best be described as Dickensian costume, aka Mr Bumble, emerged from a small, dusty clump of nettle and cow parsley. As he advanced towards us he could be seen attempting to do up the zip on his trousers, at least I sincerely hoped that was what he was doing.

"You frew that!" he shouted as he hurled the can back. "It woz delibrat and …"

The can hit the water with a dull clonk, filled slowly with brown fuel-dappled water and sank gently out of sight.

"I demands satisfaction!"

Murdock stood up and trying desperately to maintain a straight face replied, "Oh you do, do you?"

"Yes, I bleedin' well does!"

"Right!" said Murdock and jumped ship.

They faced each other across the towpath, one a good six foot in his stockinged feet and the other barely reaching the top of his navel.

"Right!" said the round, badly dressed but by now puce-coloured pygmy.

"Well go on then, hit me." Murdock pushed out his chest in a fairly good imitation of a posturing budgie and looked down on his would-be assailant.

"No, not here," came the reply.

"Well where then?" Murdock asked.

"I knows a quiet place." The little chap looked around as if expecting the girls from the Inland Revenue at the very least and laid a grimy finger to his lips.

Murdock looked helplessly back at us.

"The name's Evil Ted. Wot's yours?"

"Er … Murdock," Murdock replied, his face beginning to twitch from the strain of not laughing.

Mavis, who had been watching from the roof where she lay sprawled in a fetching, albeit faded pair of denim shorts and what could have been a top but looked more like a big bra, giggled. The malignant gnome turned and glared at her.

"Wot you laughing at?" he asked belligerently. That was before Mavis stretched, flexing her ample cleavage at the same time. He stood mesmerized and then visibly pulling himself back from whichever fantasy island he'd momentarily visited said in much more reasonable tones, "Tell you what. Why don't we 'ave a small bet on the winner?"

"What sort of bet?" Murdock asked, suddenly suspicious.

"I'll wager a hundred quid against," Evil Ted paused and ran a fat pink tongue around his lips, "one night with the tart."

Mavis uttered an extremely rude word and made a grab for the nearest sharp implement. Evil Ted watched her with interest and turning back to a now unsmiling Murdock announced thoughtfully, "Course I could make it a hundred and twenty at a pinch."

Murdock, now thoroughly unamused, narrowed his eyes and with spittle flicking from the side of a mouth full of teeth, which were now thoroughly clenched, muttered, "Anywhere will do as long as I get to jump on your bones and that I'll do for free."

"Right!"

"Right!"

"Follow me."

"Right."

And then they marched off up the towpath, Evil Ted in the lead and Murdock trailing along afterwards not unlike a grumpy brown bear being led around by its Victorian trainer. Mavis and I exchanged startled looks before locking the boat in record time and racing after them, although I noticed that Mavis had grabbed the nearest item of clothing to cover her exposed chest before we leapt overboard. We caught them up just as they were about to disappear behind a short squat concrete cube nestling at the side of the river. A rusted metal door had been set into the grey graffiti-daubed wall and it was through this that Evil Ted was leading Murdock. Suddenly sensing danger I rushed forward and grabbed the metal panel just as it was about to close, Mavis panting beside me.

Carefully we pushed it open and peered inside. A rung of steps disappeared down what looked like the neck of a concrete tunnel or large pipe. Water dripped unseen from the roof and the whole place smelt of dead cigarettes and something which had died at some point in the distant past and hadn't been buried. Sounds emanated from the cavernous depths of the pipe. Mavis and I stood in the doorway and listened.

It sounded like Epsom racecourse at the start of the first race of the season. Mavis shuddered, and then leaving the light and safety of the doorway grabbed the ladder and began to climb down into the dark. I followed, my heart knocking loudly against my ribs and the door shut. Darkness flooded in and I heard Mavis whimper on the rung below me.

Slowly we began to descend by carefully negotiating one rung at a time and as we went we noticed that it was getting lighter. At the bottom of the pipe we could almost make out another door, which was slightly ajar, and it was through the aperture of a few inches that the light was creeping.

Quietly Mavis pushed the door open and we crept out into a scene straight out of one of Murdock's sleazier books. We appeared to be in a wide brick cavern with tunnels branching off to left and right. Lining the walls were flaming torches such as you used to see in movies depicting medieval castles and mad scientists with a few optional blood-slurping human bats. We could see Murdock squaring up to Evil Ted and then as our eyes adjusted to the gloom we could also see eyes at varying levels on the periphery of the light. They appeared to be closing in on the posturing protagonists.

"Right, Ladies and Gents, this great Jessie is called Murdock and he's agreed to fight. Cos I've demanded satisfaction, see."

There was a murmur of interest from the creeping crowd and Murdock stopped weaving up and down, which was his idea of being a boxer.

"Place your bets Ladies and Gents, place your bets. I'm giving four to one against."

"Against what?" Murdock demanded.

"Against your standing up for more than one round with the Growler here."

Mavis and I exchanged horrified looks and watched with dawning terror as a figure detached itself from the side of the cavern and moved towards Murdock. He was big, at least two inches taller than our companion and built on the lines of the average troll. He also growled the sort of sound Rottweilers make before they tear out your throat.

"It's a fight," Mavis hissed at me. "Evil Ted must lure unsuspecting souls down here and then arrange for the Growler to either beat the …"

"Stuffing."

"Stuffing out of them or to let them beat him. I guess it all depends on what sort of side bets he's arranged first."

"How do you know that he might lose?" I asked, taking in the sheer size of the man.

"I did a piece on the illegal fight system."

"Hang on, didn't you have them setting up under the railway arches near the embankment?"

"Yes."

"And there was me thinking you'd made the whole thing up."

"I had."

"What."

"Shush."

In front of us the Growler was moving from side to side with Murdock avoiding him with swift dancing steps. The members of the crowd gathered around the two sweating protagonists were either groaning or clapping, depending on whether or not they had made a bet on the defeat of the by now white and grim-faced Murdock.

"Edwin."

"What?"

"You got any cash on you?"

"No. Why?"

"I was wondering about having a small bet ..."

I stared at her, dumbstruck.

"At least if he loses we can pay his medical bills."

"You're really sick," I muttered.

The Growler suddenly stopped and then raised his head and howled. Murdock stood stock-still and then with a growl that could have curdled the blood of much lesser men the Growler launched himself at Murdock. Murdock neatly sidestepped and then with the precision of an expert swung a large fist into the Growler's chin.

There was a moment of absolute silence and then the Growler folded neatly up and fell face down on the floor.

The audience roared with approval or with hoarse threats of revenge, depending on their profit or loss, and then after much noisy discussion and the collection of their winnings or the tearing-up of paper, gradually disappeared back down the far tunnels and out of sight.

When they had all moved out of earshot the Growler raised himself slowly from the floor and sat up rubbing his chin.

"How much did we make, Father?" he asked in the light treble trill of the truly homosexual and proud of it.

Mavis and I moved slowly towards the scene of recent carnage. Evil Ted watched us as we approached and smiled almost benignly.

"Did you see that?" he beamed in accents which could have graced any boat at Henley. "Absolutely bloody perfect right hook."

"Er?" Murdock stuttered, helping the Growler to his feet.

"There you are," Evil Ted announced as he passed a wad of notes over to Murdock, "your cut."

"Right." Murdock looked down at the cash in his hand.

"Sorry we can't stay and chat but I'm sure you'll understand that we need to be on our way. Can you find your own way back to the boat OK?" Evil Ted asked, collecting his jacket from a wooden pallet propped up against the wall.

"Through the door, up the ladder and turn left?" Mavis said.

"That's right sweetheart and you'll find the light switch on the right hand side above the lintel as you go through. Well must be off. Don't want to get picked up by any strange coppers, do we son?"

"No Father."

"So it's all a con?" Murdock asked, running a sweat-stained hand across his forehead.

"That's right. Got the idea from some dead poet who

writes for the Maul on Sunday."

Mavis spluttered incoherently beside me as father and son collected the last of their things. And that was that. Evil Ted and the Growler marched off down the tunnel to our right and we followed Murdock, still clutching his ill-gotten gains, back to the boat.

And that's why we were late getting through the junction at Cowley Peachy and barely made it up to the outskirts of Rickmansworth before the light went. Murdock didn't say much for the rest of that day except he offered to pay for dinner at the first hostelry we came to, after we'd tied up for the night. But as we fell into our respective beds at the end of the day he suddenly said in tones of perplexed approval.

"Bleedin' two hundred quid, who says crime doesn't pay?"

chapter fourteen

Stowaways!

We awoke to something which sounded like the evil mastermind the Penguin having a fight with either Batman or Robin. Murdock shouted something fairly rude and pulled a pillow over his head, as Mavis and I cautiously passed him on the way to the continuing sounds of disturbance. It was five thirty in the morning and even the sun was having problems getting up. Mavis slowly opened the door to the front deck armed with a hastily collected kitchen utensil and I skulked behind her as back-up.

What greeted our sleep-encrusted eyes was a family of scruffy ducks who had decided to take up residence in our spare washing-up bowl. Mavis turned to me with a relieved grin and muttered, "I soiled my armour for that?"

"Well at least you came prepared." I pointed wolfishly at the pan in her hand and licked my lips. "Do we have any oranges?"

"You're sick, you know that," Mavis replied as we moved back to the relative warmth of the boat.

"Might as well get dressed and start the engine as we're up," she announced with a yawn.

"All right," I muttered and went back to my bunk for some clothes.

Mavis now had my old berth in the centre of the boat and I now had the fold-away bed above the double bed at the end. Murdock had the bottom as he was built on more generous lines and the top berth wasn't exactly large. His excuse for taking the lower one was officially that of having had vertigo from a tender and unspecified age. I privately thought it had more to do with an inability to climb when inebriated but moved my stuff anyway with out too much whingeing. 'After all,' I'd muttered mutinously, as I'd cleared the cupboard under the bottom berth, 'Mother has always instilled in me a respect for the old and infirm.' Murdock had tried to cuff my ears but I was faster and ran away.

Ten minutes later I stood behind Mavis, clutching a mug of coffee and a slab of toast, which dripped butter onto the dew-encrusted deck, as we watched the early morning world slip by. There was the occasional call of a bird and the distant hum of lorries from nearby roads which crossed and wriggled their way around the canal.

Somewhere on the far side of the surrounding hedges and tall banks of waving grasses, a horse whinnied to another of its kind. With a gentle putt-putter, the wash from the *Maybole Rose* wetly kissed the hulls of the other sleeping barges, rocking them gently as we passed. There were no other vessels around and so Mavis allowed me to steer. I began after an hour to get the hang of the thing and suddenly realized we had managed to negotiate a small bridge without hitting the sides or the bank as we floated safely out from under the shadowed brick walls.

Murdock eventually emerged at about nine, rubbing his eyes and clutching a Murdock Special, which he downed in one.

"The secret," he announced on seeing our horrified faces as he drank deeply of the loathsome mix, "is to add just the right touch of Worcestershire sauce."

"That and having no taste buds left," Mavis hissed at me as Murdock clambered back down into the boat, shutting the hatch as he went.

The rest of the day passed peaceably enough with the three of us taking hourly turns on the helm, except for the navigation of the next ladder of locks, all twenty-nine of them, when Mavis steered and Murdock and I used our combined expertise and brute strength to open them.

We finally arrived at Berkhamsted at about five thirty and while Mavis went off to find some fresh supplies Murdock and I were left to tie up and sort out our newly acquired squatters. Or at least that was the theory. What Murdock and I actually did was to make a pot of tea, load it on to an old gaily decorated tin tray and then we scuttled off to the far end of the boat to discuss our next move.

"Well," Murdock announced after a gulp of hot tannin, "I reckon we ought to creep up behind them with the boat hook and tip the bowl over the side."

And that's what we did. Unfortunately the ducks had left a particularly vicious drake we had named Mad Erik on lookout patrol. We crept around the side of the cabin door and Mad Erik attacked from the roof. There was a nasty moment when I was in serious danger of losing an eye, but Murdock beat him off with a wet towel before stitches were required.

Mavis returned laden down with fresh bread, eggs, sausages and two pints of milk to find feathers all over the deck and Murdock applying plasters to the gash under my right eye. Mad Erik glared at us from the television aerial we'd wired up next to the roof ventilator above the galley, and the other ducks had gone back to squatting in the washing-up bowl. Mavis shook her head at the pair of us but despite the rude mouthing of the word 'cowards' she still boarded the boat from the back end.

We waited for her to come up with a more brilliant method of pest control by downing a beer each, and the world began to take on a sunnier glow as we opened our second and Mavis returned clutching the Observer's book of birds, a small moth-eaten paperback which we'd found stuffed under the sofa.

"Well," I asked, "Does it have any tips on how to remove our feathered stowaways?"

"Not really. It did point out that some species get very territorial. I reckon that Mad Erik is the dominant male and …"

There was a muttered "You don't say" from Murdock, who was still seething quietly in the far corner.

"And the others are his wives and children."

"*Wives* – no wonder he's half mad."

Mavis glared icily at Murdock.

"Perhaps he's just quackers," I giggled. Beer does funny things to my system including my brain's desire to make very juvenile jokes.

Mavis and Murdock exchanged a look of pained patience.

"Oh, I've had enough of this!" Mavis suddenly announced and marched off down to the front of the boat, armed with the remains of the baguette we'd almost devoured at lunchtime.

"Perhaps," Murdock stated, "she's going to beat Erik up with the really hard bit at the end?"

We watched as she approached the family of ducks and knelt out of sight. We waited. There was a short period of loud quacks and Erik launched himself from the roof. Murdock and I clambered from the *Maybole Rose* and carefully crept along the towpath to where we could see Mavis squatting down next to the bowl, Erik standing to attention behind her. Mavis stood up as we approached, smoothing large crumbs of bread from her jeans.

"You'll be pleased to know that we have reached a working agreement."

The ducks nodded their mottled heads and fixed Murdock and I with black beady eyes.

"Brunhilde," Mavis pointed to the very large fat brown duck sitting in the centre of the bowl, "has laid some eggs and the ducks will remain with us until they've hatched. In return they will stand guard over the boat while we're off downing a few well earned pints."

"Er?"

"Any questions?" Mavis asked, her face set.

"How do we know they won't go for us again?" I asked, my cheek still throbbing.

"Because they've given me their word," Mavis replied, jumping down to join us.

Murdock and I stood and looked from Mad Erik, who was now marching up and down the bow, to Mavis.

"Potty," was all Murdock said as he clambered back on board to grab some cash and to lock up.

Two hours later we arrived back to find our lodgers gently sleeping, beaks tucked under wings. Erik opened one eye and glared at us in the time-honoured way of all parents who would resort to violence if faced with the prospect of anybody waking their offspring.

It had been a funny sort of day, I thought as I sipped my mug of Ovaltine and watched the moon struggling to break through the branches of an old withered elm which overhung the canal bank on the opposite side. I looked around at the silver- flecked world and realized that I really didn't miss my old life at all. Well, maybe bits of it. Long hot deep baths and freshly laundered clothes and maybe a shave once in a while. I rubbed the stubble on my chin, which was trying to become something more than just a brown shadow. One day, I promised myself, you will become the owner of a beard, one of those smart hairy things other men can get away with.

Something jumped on my foot. It was Erik. Cautiously I held out the last remains of a shortbread biscuit. Erik dipped his head and devoured the crumbs. I regarded my remaining fingers and carefully counted them. All ten were still there. I remembered old pantomimes I'd been to as a child where the villain was always threatened with some form of punishment, one of them being that he'd be nibbled to death by ducks. Looking at Erik I could see why it was something you'd spend a fair amount of time avoiding.

"Nice evening," I said, anxious to break the silence.

"Quack," agreed Erik.

That night I dreamt that I had become Pip, from *Great Expectations*. Murdock was rowing me out to sea in a boat, the police were hot on our trail and keeping watch with a long silver telescope was Mr Micawber, who turned as I watched into a large brown and green duck with a pair of raisin-black gimlet eyes.

chapter fifteen

Hairy Mary and the three witches

"Morning Erik," I gaily stated the next day after having brushed my teeth and discovered that I almost had a moustache. I'd always wanted one and although it wasn't exactly your average Hercule Poirot, being at least three inches shorter, it did look deliberate and not merely as if I had forgotten to shave.

"Look," I advised Mavis, who was mauling eggs in a bowl. She looked up from fishing shell out with her fingers and wrinkled her nose in thought.

"You look," she observed slowly, "like a dodgy car dealer."

"Do I? Do I really?" I asked, gleefully bouncing. At last I'd stopped looking like an apprentice mechanic – instead I now resembled his boss.

Mavis shook her head and went back to her culinary duties.

Murdock was sitting on the sofa reading one of Brian

Roberts's books on the waterways of Britain and trying to work out where we should tie up for the night.

"I missed the Ovaltine works," he morosely muttered.

"Oh."

"Again."

"Right."

"I always miss it."

"There are films like that."

"Yep."

"Do you remember *Lord of the Rings* part three?"

"Good film that."

"Well I've never managed to watch all of it in one go; I've seen the beginning and the end but not the middle. Then I managed to get all the way through and missed the last half an hour."

"That used to happen with me. My bête noire was an old Bette Davis classic *Now Voyager*."

"Who?"

Murdock gave me one of his looks.

"Never mind, little grasshopper."

I grinned back at him. I had no idea who the little grasshopper was but the allusion always cheered Murdock up, so I never let on. I had asked Mavis but she just stared at me as if she couldn't really believe I really didn't know. The trouble with journalists was that they were almost literate and knew an awful lot of obscure things ordinary mortals wouldn't have given houseroom to.

"So," I asked. "What delights do we pass today?"

"Well," Murdock poured over his map again and stabbed parts of it with a stubby finger, "there's the Tring Cutting."

"Where?"

"Here. Seven thousand foot long and thirty foot deep,

straight as an arrow through the Chilterns."

"Anything else?" I asked, flexing my toes.

"The Great Ouse Aqueduct. You'll enjoy that. It was built in 1811 from a lot of iron bits. That was because the previous brick one, built three years earlier, collapsed. Which is why I'm going to cook lunch." Murdock shuddered at the thought of all that water travelling that high up, on something built that long ago.

Mavis, with perfect timing, appeared armed with plates piled high with slabs of toast and mottled scrambled egg. Mugs of tea followed and we began to eat in a peaceful silence punctuated by the occasional crunch as we found the bits of eggshell, which had managed to escape the sifting process.

Afterwards we cast off without any mishap and set off for the aqueduct. Mavis had serious doubts about our reaching it that day, and after looking at our chart so did I. But as Murdock was obviously winding himself up for a great disaster we decided to keep quiet. As it was Murdock prepared lunch as we navigated the Tring Cutting and by the end of that day we had managed to get as far north as Fenny Stratford.

We moored up just past the lock, which according to Murdock had been built by mistake. I wasn't sure how you could build anything that big by mistake and then I remembered the Greater London Olympic Stadium, now a water park and educational resource.

There was a pub called 'The Hairy Mary' a mere matter of yards from the boat, which Murdock assured us did the best duck in orange he'd ever had, which was perhaps not exactly the most tactful thing to say when your security officer was a demented member of the same fraternity. Erik gave us the evil eye and as we gingerly sidled past his perch of the day, both Mavis and I promised to have the steak.

'The Hairy Mary' was one of those old timbered hostelries that welcome you with promises of real beer and good food and then add on things like quiz nights and karaoke. Luckily we had picked a night where the only thing on offer was a man who could play the saw and someone billed as 'Alma the amazing Amazon'. Alma, a lady of uncertain years, according to the old boy sitting in the inglenook nursing a large brown drink which smoked gently, did something with a large green snake nicknamed Hannibal the Cannibal.

Mavis muttered something that sounded like. "Oh goodie, culture, can't wait," before settling herself into a high-backed bench seat near the window.

The pub was quietly empty and the only person sitting near us was a large woman draped in a shawl and a lot of black baggy garments. The shawl was a fascinating riot of colours with a sort of metallic mesh woven into a haphazard pattern of dragons and garishly ornate chrysanthemums.

Occasionally she'd look up from the book she was studying to glance at the door. Just as our starter arrived something small, thin and resembling an old walnut with legs scuttled in through the front door and sat down in the corner next to her.

"Well?" the shawl asked, laying the book aside.

"Well what?"

"Did you get it?"

"Sort of – and before you start, Felicity, I'll have a port and lemon with lots of ice – I'm that parched."

The shawl grunted and moved off to the bar, returning a

few minutes later with a large ruby red drink in a balloon glass and a pint of something black.

"So where is it?"

"There."

A plastic lunchbox was shoved onto the table and the shawl had a good look inside. There was a short silence, while I spread pate on triangles of brown toast, Murdock chased melon balls round his plate and Mavis fished around in her dish for the last pinkly smothered prawn

"It looks like a chicken fillet and a bit of chopped liver." The shawl remarked.

"Well that's because it is."

"Ah."

"Difficult to get Fenny snake, especially out of season. Our Dawn had something they said was snake in Hong Kong once and she said it tasted just like chicken, so I got a nice bit of fillet from the butcher and he threw in some liver as well. There was a kidney too but the dog had it."

"Well, I suppose it will have to do."

Mavis choked on her prawn and while I patted her on the back, a third woman arrived, dressed in a very smart green tweed suit and a Liberty print scarf.

"Thrice the brinded cat hath mewed," she muttered, sitting down.

"Thrice and once the hedge-pig whined," croaked the walnut.

"Harpier cries ''tis time, 'tis time'. Want the usual, Ethel?" Ethel must have nodded because the shawl got up and went back to the bar.

Murdock looked into the nearly empty bottom of his glass and stared eloquently at Mavis much as Erik did when he saw anything edible which wasn't actively being ingested.

Mavis, who had by now recovered from her coughing fit, collected our now empty glasses and lurched off to the bar.

"What's in the box?" Ethel asked.

"Fillet of a Fenny snake and a bit of liver from a blaspheming Jew. Couldn't get a Turk's nose though and I'm having a bit of bother with the finger of birth-strangled babe."

"Did you have a word with Dr Mitforth?"

"Went to see her when I picked up our Henry's prescription for that new Viagra but she said she didn't have anything in. She said she'd have a word with a friend down at the Path Lab but she wasn't all that hopeful."

"Oh well, I managed to get most of the rest. Think that will do, 'for the toad that under cold stone days and nights has thirty one?'"

"It's a bit chewed."

"Yeah, but from a distance?"

Murdock and I exchanged speaking glances and then sat back in our respective seats in order to hear a bit better.

"That's plastic," the shawl pointed out as she lowered herself back into her seat.

"No one will notice if we throw it in quick," Ethel pointed out.

There was the sound of a plastic bag being rummaged through and then a series of delighted 'Oohs' as the contents were carefully inspected.

Mavis returned at that point and whispered.

"You are not going to believe what I've just seen."

"Shush," admonished Murdock.

"I managed to salvage the eye of newt and toe of frog from the Zoology Lab but I'm afraid I couldn't get hold of anything which even resembled a blind worm's sting."

"Of course you couldn't!" exclaimed the walnut. "He made that bit up."

"Oh?"

"I mean he had to rhyme the bit about the lizard's leg and owlet's wing."

Our duck in orange arrived at that point together with a large dish of vegetables and another of fat golden chips. We looked down on our plates, our appetites temporarily mislaid.

"You eating then?" the shawl asked.

"Don't mind if I do – doubt if we'll get much time to get anything tomorrow. Especially if that wretched cauldron plays up again."

"I blame that ponce Derek, he's always putting in too much of that dry ice."

"And the bang last week. Talk about over the top. And what about poor old Ernie, all he came to do was to fix the lights and now look at him!"

"He'll feel much better when he gets his cast off," the shawl murmured in a soothing fashion before adding thoughtfully, "and to be absolutely fair he didn't know anyone was on top of that ladder."

"Its Shirley's fault. That woman couldn't organize a night out at a brothel if you threw in a couple of inflatables and a set of manacles. Right then, I'll have the duck."

"Nice bit of liver and onions for me."

"I'll have the Chicken Kiev. Timothy's gone to some old boy reunion at Aylesbury, so there'll be no one home to notice the smell." Ethel rose and tottered off to give in their order, her wedge-shaped heels tapping loudly across the wooden floor.

"To be honest I don't know why we bother. Malcolm

still doesn't know his lines and who ever heard of a six foot ten Macbeth with blonde hair and a nose stud?"

"Moira knows all her lines." the shawl declared in accents of barely disguised loathing.

"Yeah, but she looks like a performing plank. That bit when she says 'out damm spot', looks like she's putting the cat out for the night."

"Mind you, it's the costumes that really worry me."

"Aye."

"I mean, whoever heard of frilly witches?"

"I look like a lampshade, a pink one."

"Well ladies, it's all set." Ethel had returned beaming from ear to ear. "I've just had a word with young Roger behind the bar and he says we can borrow some of the choir's old hassocks. The ones they had made for that production of the Crucifixion. You remember, the smart black ones with the hoods and the scarlet lining that the vicar said made him look like a Hogwart's supply teacher?"

"Well done," said the shawl, banging her glass down on the table.

"I'll drink to that," agreed the walnut.

"Ladies, I would like to propose a toast."

"Please do."

"To us. May we be bloody, bold and resolute!" There was the sound of clinking glasses and the hasty gulping of liquid.

The front door slammed open against the wall and a slim, harassed-looking, middle-aged woman with teeth like a horse and long black hair dragged back into a ponytail marched in. With a porcine squeal of recognition she spied the threesome in the corner and pounced.

"What the hell are you lot doing here?"

"Evening Jemima, do you want a drink?" the walnut asked.

"No I don't want a drink! Don't you know you should be down at the hall?"

"No we don't, because according to the rehearsal sheets that you drew up, we are officially off tonight, while you rehearse the Macbeths for their final scene."

"They didn't turn up. Allan had to work late."

"Well we didn't know that, did we?" the shawl uttered in accents of stolid reasonableness.

"No, I suppose not." There was a pause interrupted by the arrival of their food.

"Wouldn't you like a bit of extra practice with that cauldron?" Jemima asked in tones of saccharin sweetness.

"No we bloody well wouldn't, we are having our tea. Now bugger off and do something useful." Ethel hissed, cutting into her chicken.

"Like drowning that two-faced tit you put in charge of props," the walnut muttered.

Jemima left to the sounds of raucous cackling and the three witches, by now in a very much sunnier frame of mind, tucked into their well-earned dinner.

Mavis, Murdock and myself finished our respective meals and toyed with the idea of pudding. However, as even Murdock admitted with a last long and loving look at the dessert menu, if we ate any more we would probably sink the *Maybole*, so we opted to err on the side of caution and ordered a large pot of coffee and three cups.

Mavis toddled off to the ladies while we waited, and upon her return she threw a small black and white poster onto the table. It informed us that the Bletchley Players were performing the Scottish play for three nights only at the village hall in aid of the local school and the church organ fund.

"It's tomorrow night," Mavis said. "Couldn't we stay here an extra day? I haven't seen a play for ages." Murdock and I looked at each other. I could tell that Murdock was wavering – he'd be able to put off the great aerial disaster for a further day.

"All right," he agreed.

"Edwin?" Mavis looked pleadingly at me.

"OK," I agreed. A whole day off: I could give my blisters a well deserved and much needed rest. We could even find a launderette and track down a friendly boatyard with the tools and pumping equipment necessary to sort out the toilet. It had started 'acting up' again, according to Mavis. Murdock said all it needed was a good kick but then as Mavis had hissed to me later, Murdock's boat had been so well maintained it had sunk.

Later that same evening as I slowly brushed my teeth, I stared happily at my hairy reflection. A whole day off – I could sleep in and I'd have another day of facial growth. Maybe tomorrow would be the day that I'd finally be able to unleash the moustache on an unsuspecting world.

chapter sixteen

A grand day out

I awoke at ten the next morning and stretched in the snug confines of my duvet. The sun shone brightly, hailing a day of warmth and laziness. There was absolutely no need to get up so I rolled over and closed my eyes for another half hour. It was Murdock who woke me next with a steaming cup of tea.

"Get up, you lazy sod," he mumbled as he deposited the tea on the shelf next to my head and ambled off to the bathroom, having a general scratch at the hairs poking from between the buttons of his pyjama top as he went.

By half past eleven Mavis had departed for the nearest launderette with our briefly sorted washing, Murdock had gone to see a man about the toilet and I was left to make the sandwiches for lunch and to sort the health hazard out: the health hazard being the dropping-encrusted, feather-lined, rather fruity-smelling washing-up bowl. I had, after due consideration, opted for neat disinfectant around the bowl area and I'd managed to brush and wash the worst of the duck poo off the side of the bowl with a long-handled mop.

Erik had watched from the roof for even the slightest sign of assault and had then jumped down and relieved himself all over the freshly cleaned bit.

"Erik!" I shouted as I washed the deck down again.

Mavis found me standing guard with a large broom and a bottle of anti-fungal spray at the ready as the varnished wood surface dried in the sun. We had discovered quite by accident that Erik hated the smell of the lemon kitchen cleaner, without the timely discovery of which Erik would by now be sleeping indoors.

"Papers!" Mavis called as she threw them on the saloon table.

I lit the gas and put the kettle on as she doled out clean washing from the two plastic bags she'd dragged back with her. And then while the kettle boiled I carefully stowed my clean clothes away after sniffing them first. Murdock arrived back in time to find me with my snout buried in a pair of underpants.

"Strange lad," he muttered in passing.

"We have to shift the *Maybole* up to the yard and Dudley will have a look at it," he announced, biting into a cheese and chutney sandwich. "Kettle's burning nicely," he added.

I raced up to the galley and turned the gas off, just as the last drop of water vaporised.

"I thought all them jokes about men that were so useless they could burn water were old wives' tales," he muttered, spraying crumbs across the lounge.

I filled the kettle again and went back to the table. I picked up one of the papers and aimlessly turned the pages until I got to page eight where my own face stared straight back at me.

"Bloody hell!" I croaked, sitting down abruptly.

"What you done now?" Murdock asked, reading over my shoulder before getting up to take charge of the coffee.

"Listen to this – listen!" I spluttered, my eyes straining from their sockets in numb disbelief. 'Edwin Snipe, the most wanted man in Britain, has been seen at an Arab camp in Bosnia. Edwin, wanted in connection with the recent attempted murder of Ms Harriet Smith-Patel, manager of WH Smiths, Dock Ten, London Central, has managed to evade capture by joining up with anti-management forces in Europe. This paper has assiduously campaigned for tighter controls over travel to and from the lands of smelly cheese and smoked sausage and now feels vindicated with the ease with which Mr Snipe has managed to rejoin his degenerate friends. And there's a picture. Look!"

I handed the paper over to Murdock who gave it a fairly dispassionate glance before taking another bite out of his sandwich.

"Ah well, you know the press, lad. If they manage to spell your name right you're lucky."

"But …" I gurgled. Murdock patted me on the head and then began to chew slowly on a large yellow pickled onion.

Mavis sauntered in, picked up the paper, gave it a cursory look and moved off to dump her empty plate in the sink.

"Mavis!" I squeaked. " Have you seen what your erstwhile employer has done!"

"Seen it, Sweetie? I wrote it."

Murdock and I stared at her in the sort of stunned way fish do when they've been electrocuted.

"Pardon?" we bleated in unison.

"I wrote it. What do you think I've been doing every morning and evening when I go to the shops? I've been ringing that in. You've done the whole thing: escaped out to sea on an inflatable shark, got picked up by French fishing boat, followed by a perilous journey across France and other foreign parts. The pictures aren't bad though. We had some young Lionel had taken at one of them fancy government garden parties. Don't you remember? You attended in a sort of fancy Arab dress complete with overhead tablecloth and embroidered curly-toed slippers. All we did was to digitally impose a different background and stick in a couple of terrorists with semi-automatics. Looks good though."

"But why?" I asked, as my shattered reputation lay in tatters around me.

"Because if you're in Europe you can't be here, which means that no one is looking too hard for you. Good grief Edwin, why do you think we've had no one asking awkward questions? Why the police aren't patrolling the towpaths? It is because I, Mavis Wordsworth, have publicly told them not to bother."

"And because you're still up to your usual poisonous perambulations they aren't looking for you either," Murdock stated, spearing another onion from the large jar he'd bought in one of the organic farm shops we'd passed near Kings Langley.

"Exactly."

Ah well, the reputation might be in small pieces but at least I was relatively safe, my brain told my ego.

Erik waddled in and looked at us hopefully. It was like having a small-feathered dog without having to take him for walks. Murdock offered him an onion, which was received with the calculated disdain of the truly spoiled. Mavis proffered a cheese and bacon crisp which was nibbled with gusto and we eventually persuaded him to leave by throwing the end of that day's supply of rolls over the side.

That evening I sat at the back of the local village hall and watched one of the worst and at the same time funniest productions of the Scottish play I'd ever seen. We rolled our way back to the *Maybole Rose* still clutching our sides some two hours after the event. We'd been invited backstage by the witches for the end of run party, which had been brought forward two days as the castle interior set had collapsed, the director had fled the village with much wailing and gnashing of teeth and the vicar had double-booked the hall. No one really minded as they all looked forward to the annual Brownie, Guide and Scout barn dance. No one mentioned the Cubs so perhaps they'd been banned?

Macbeth, who could have played Richard the third without the need of the costume and make-up department, had lisped his way through the play. Lady Macbeth had come on and performed the sleepwalking scene complete with a cloud of alcohol and her knickers showing. She'd obviously been in the bathroom before her entrance was called and hadn't pulled her skirt back down. Halfway through the witches' big scene the plastic cauldron had melted and half the set had gone up in a wall of smoke. The woods of Dunsinane consisted of two lads with a couple of Christmas tree branches, and Duncan's toupee had fallen off.

All in all, the sort of production that carried all before it – only I had a feeling that the deaf prompt was going to be sacked as soon as the producer could track her down. Either that or she was going to be impaled on some of the wicked-looking spikes that the guards had been carrying around with them all evening.

The witches came back to the boat with us as Murdock

and Mavis considered our position quite safe, and we managed to polish off the last of the malt whisky, together with a small bottle of brandy Murdock had found in his sock drawer.

It was three in the morning before we finally tumbled into our beds. I sat and stared drunkenly at the shadows and reflections of silver rippling across the ceiling above my head and finally felt almost free. I snuggled down under the covers and thanked the big boss upstairs for all the things I'd up to that point taken for granted and in particular for the freedom of the press, who could, I now knew, write anything they damm well liked and every word would be digested by the great reading public and totally believed.

chapter seventeen

The man in the brown suit

I was awoken the next day by a loud crackling noise. At first I blearily wondered whether someone had stuck my head in a bowl of Rice Krispies and had then poured milk over the top. Murdock groaned in the bunk below. Slowly I came to and gingerly raised my head. The boat was oddly dark and silent. I had the sudden awful thought that Erik had been ducknapped and would be on somebody's plate by suppertime, so, grabbing an old top I opened up the stern hatch and staggered out into the gloom.

Great drops of water flew at me from every direction and I staggered back indoors.

"What's up?" Murdock asked. "What swine put the lights out?"

"No one, it's raining."

"Raining?"

"Yeah."

"How hard?"

"Start with downpour and then work up towards

monsoon," I replied, lurching into my trousers and a pair of socks.

"Ah well, look on the bright side – at least our Erik will be happy. Ducks like rain."

I wasn't convinced. I'd glimpsed something dark green and soggy cowering under the stern light before I'd slammed the door. Mind you, in my present state it was probably just an old scrap of rubbish.

Half an hour later I was munching toast and looking out of the window at a grey vista: grey trees, grey towpath, grey grass, grey water and a lot of grey sky, when there was a loud thump on the front door. I ignored it and poured myself another mug of coffee. But the door clanged again, this time much louder and with vibrations.

"What was that?" Mavis asked blearily, peering out from the shower room.

"Don't know," I replied, reaching for the marmalade.

"Well, go and see!" she exploded, the towel that had been almost covering her slipping from mildly erotic to downright obscene.

Muttering dark oaths of a biblical nature, I cautiously opened the door and something small and wet shot between my legs. It was Erik.

"Morning Erik," I said.

"Quack" came the reply and Erik shook himself like a dog, water shooting off in all directions.

"Wet enough for you?" I asked.

Erik glared at me and clicked his beak.

I went back to my toast and Erik waddled up and sat beside me. There was a tea towel lying across the back of the seat, so I tucked it around his waterlogged form and gave him a small piece of toast. We sat in a companionable silence as the rain lashed the deck and hammered at the windows.

"Who was it?" Mavis asked, now fully dressed, as she stuck some bread under the grill.

"What?"

"Outside."

"Post," I replied. Erik looked up at me with black beady eyes; he knew, as I did, that Mavis had very strong opinions on animals and animals indoors in particular. I carefully covered him completely in the towel and went back to staring out of the window.

"Post?"

"What?"

"Oh, forget it," Mavis snapped back.

Mavis finished cremating her breakfast and arrived at my elbow clutching a plate of embers and a mug.

"Budge up," she demanded.

I moved slowly further down the seat, giving Erik the opportunity to drop onto the floor and to hide under my legs. We would have been all right if Mavis hadn't have dropped a piece of charred bread with extra marmalade. It had a large piece of orange peel attached to it and as Mavis bent to pick it up Erik went to spear it with his beak. There was a deathly hush as they both put on the brakes at the same time.

"Erik!"

"Quack?"

"Outside!"

Mavis frogmarched the cowering creature to the door and flung it open. Water fell in a solid sheet onto her unprotected head and with the speed and agility of a scorpion she slammed it shut and leant against it. Water dripped onto the floor and Erik, after giving her one of his best told-you-so looks, jumped back onto the seat, flicked the tea towel over his back with his beak, stuck his head over his folded wings and closed one eye.

"What about Brunhilde and the egg?" I asked.

Mavis peered out of the oval side window and scanned the deck.

"She's gone," Mavis replied.

"Gone?" I joined her at the window and stared out into the rain. The washing-up bowl, now nearly full of mucky water was empty of ducks. The deck was clear apart from a few soggy feathers and a scattering of what I suddenly realized was eggshell, bluish-green eggshell with speckles.

Mavis and I looked at each other.

"Fox?" I mouthed at her.

"Dunno," she mouthed back.

We both turned and regarded Erik with solemnity.

"Sorry Erik," we croaked.

"Quack," Erik replied and closed both eyes.

An hour later we all donned thick yellow waterproofs, and looking like a collection of North sea fishermen, cast off and lumbered down the canal, which was now complete with small waves, although they felt a hell of a lot bigger in a flat-bottomed craft where the windows were only a foot above the waterline.

We took turns to steer, and luckily there were only nine locks to go before our evening berth, so we did have occasion to thaw out between bursts of energy. The Great Ouse Aqueduct was passed over in a sheet of dank water vapour so I completely missed its magnificence. After nine hours we eventually arrived at Stoke Bruerne; wet, cold and in desperate need of warm clothes and hot food. Water dribbled down my neck and my hands, almost blue with cold, fumbled hopelessly with the water tap as I tried to attach our water hose on the end. The metal clip kept slipping and I couldn't release the valve. Tears of frustration welled up as Murdock joined me. Pushing me gently to one side, he adroitly fixed the two ends together and turned the tap. Nothing happened. Outraged, he kicked it. A man throwing something from a saucepan over the side of his boat a few yards down shouted, "That bugger don't work, try the other one further along." He pointed to a small sign hammered into the ground about a hundred yards further along the canal.

Murdock thanked him and with much f'ing and blinding, we wearily untied all the ropes, started the engine, scrambled back on board and went through the whole wet and cold routine of tying up and trying to fill the water tank again.

No one felt like leaving the *Maybole* that night, so Murdock prepared his very own recipe for boat stew. I watched in fascination as he emptied a large can of stewing steak in gravy into the bottom of our largest and oldest pan. There followed a can of tomatoes, mixed vegetables, potatoes, corn, butter beans and finally one of baked beans. Murdock stirred it all up and then left it to brew quietly for about twenty minutes. Mavis and I looked into the reddish coloured concoction we'd been presented with and then tentatively lifted a bit out with our forks and nibbled it. I'm not sure if Murdock did anything else while we weren't looking but it was one of the best onboard meals I'd had.

In honour of his culinary prowess Mavis opened up a bottle of red wine from some obscure European country and we ate in companionable silence, the rain drumming a light Scottish reel on the roof as we bumped gently against the bank. Outside the wind had picked up and Erik, after being forced outside to do the sort of things that ducks had to do, was allowed back indoors as long as he kept to his newly washed out bowl, lined with newspaper and his favourite towel.

I was watching a late night film on television when Erik got up and quacked loudly at the door, and thinking that he needed to go, I opened it and looked out. Something moved quickly into the bushes lining the canalside, something brown.

"Bloody fox," I muttered.

With a start I remembered the pathetically small collection of shell pieces we'd found scattered around the deck that morning, and enraged, I pulled on my Wellingtons and oilskin coat and jumped ashore. Erik, ever curious, followed in my wake, like a small tug caught in the slipstream of a very angry supertanker.

I carefully edged my way into the bushes and just as I was about to launch myself into the space on the other side, I was firmly hauled back and pushed to the ground. Murdock loomed over me and with his finger to his lips carefully shoved past me to stare intently at the woods beyond.

I stared up at him; well not just at him; the small gun firmly held in his right hand was taking up most of my attention.

"Stay absolutely bloody still," Murdock whispered.

Lights flashed in the gloom and in their long beams I could see a man in a brown suit. The lights suddenly went out and an engine rumbled into life. Murdock grabbed me and together we crawled back to the boat.

Shaking, I slithered on board. Murdock hastily dashed down the entire length switching off all the lights. The rain was beginning to ease up and a faint moon glowed above the trees.

"Murdock, what's happened?" Mavis asked and then she saw the gun.

"No time to explain. Just help me start the engine and cast off."

"But we can't travel at night," I said, regarding him helplessly.

"If you want to live to see the morning you're going to bloody well have to," Murdock urged, throwing Mavis her oilskins.

Mavis and I exchanged looks of mutual horror and moved, galvanized into action not by the metal shape in his hand but the intense and very serious expression on Murdock's face.

Later as we slowly negotiated our way north I asked Murdock who the man in the brown suit was.

"Somebody I once worked with," Murdock replied, squinting into the layered dark.

"Oh."

"Somebody I was told was dead, somebody who I believe killed your father."

"How?"

"Never mind how, we've plenty of time to discuss that. What we have to do now is reach the Gayton Junction. I can contact someone there who can put us up for the night and then we have to somehow get up to Coventry before they realize we've left the canal."

"But …"

"Edwin, do you want to see the sunrise?"

"Yes."

"Then stop asking bloody silly questions and pack."

chapter eighteen

The face at the window

The only thing I really remember about that night was the silence. Mavis never argued once; it was as if whatever it was that had put the fear of God into Murdock, had done the same to her. Neither of them spoke much, they just whispered sparingly and did a lot of hand movements. Even Erik kept quiet as he sat hunched up in the bow keeping watch.

Large industrial barges and other commercial vessels passed us, their bow waves catching the *Maybole* in flashes of silver and black. It isn't until you travel by night with few lights that you realize how many shades of black there are. I thought I'd seen most until we hit the tunnel: it was like entering the gates of Hell only a lot colder. Black stretched on forever. Water dripped unseen from the roof, which glowered over our heads hidden in the gloom and dank air above. I shuddered as I pictured the poor souls who had had to literally walk the old barges along these tunnels, their backs breaking and their legs caked in the mud and algae that covered the glistening brick walls in a thin layer of sooty slime.

The only lights we had showing were the ones needed for navigation and they glowed eerily back at us from the water below and the rounded roof above. Occasionally we came across an air vent let into the space above us; we'd hear the sound first before we reached it, and even with the engine churning the loud surge of falling water made my imagination run riot. Visions of dark sluices and the boiling pools beneath the falls I'd seen once on a trip to Switzerland, leapt out and glued themselves onto my inner eye. I knew it was illogical but old fairy tales and ghost stories I'd read as a child kept coming back to me. I could almost hear my mother's voice as she read me the tale of the water imps who haunted the dark unfathomable places of the underworld and dragged living creatures down to their watery graves. I shuddered and wrapped myself further into my coat.

A pinprick of light became visible at the end of the tunnel. At first I thought it was the entrance until I realized it wasn't yet time for the sun to raise a bleary eyelid.

The light grew nearer and I could hear the mechanical "chug, chug" of another engine.

Mavis and Murdock turned the *Maybole* into the tunnel side, the gears moved down to crawl. There wasn't a lot of room for two boats to pass comfortably and so erring on the side of caution was a prudent move, especially as we had no idea how experienced the approaching helmsman was.

It seemed to take forever before we could clearly see the outline of the other boat. White mist encircled the hull making it appear like a ghost ship as it finally emerged from the surrounding gloom. Yellow lights glowered from the interior and we could clearly see figures moving inside. Suddenly Murdock appeared from his vantage point hunched up in the bow and pushed me to the ground for the second time that evening.

The other barge drew level and then away as we passed, the wash from each vessel mingling in a flurry of silver and gold with spots and pools of red and green. I looked up and clearly reflected in the saloon window was a face staring right at us. I whimpered and Murdock hastily covered my mouth with an oily hand.

When the other barge had become a faint round of light behind us, Murdock allowed me to sit up. I rubbed my legs and stamped deadened feet as the circulation returned in waves of painful prickles.

"That was Mr Warwick," I muttered.

"Yes," Murdock replied and carefully closing the curtains around the galley, fumbled for a match and lit the gas.

"I think we could all do with a nice cup of tea," he announced, and passed a hand across his face, wiping the water that had collected on his skin onto his thick woollen-gloved hand.

Later as we sat looking out at the darkness with the dawn just breaking in ribbons of red and electric blue, Murdock finally explained exactly who he really was.

"I don't suppose you remember much about the times before the New Management, apart from what they allowed into those so-called history books of yours," Murdock asked. I shook my head and shrugged: History as taught by the New Management had never been one of my strong points.

"I was twenty-five," Murdoch continued, "when the twin towers were blown and the world changed; I can even remember where I was." His face blanked and some very strong emotion passed through his eyes and was then blinked away. "Thousands died and then even more died afterwards. For a while everyone remembered why we had a war against terrorists and why we'd helped invade Afghanistan and Iraq, that is until too many soldiers died and the refugees began to surge in from Europe and the old Soviet Bloc countries. The woolly-minded liberals started bleating about human rights and fair play. Fair play – what kind of idealistic crap is it that gives some bastard the right to use children as bombs?" He paused and rummaged around in his pocket until he found a long blackened cigar and a lighter. I watched in fascination as he lit the end and took a long hard pull of acrid smoke.

"You smoke," I observed, slightly awed.

"Only cigars."

I'd never seen him smoke before, and apart from it being totally illegal I wondered where he'd managed to buy the cigar in the first place.

"What happened?" Mavis asked, her journalistic nose twitching like a rabbit's before a field of radishes. "And don't try to con me, we all know about September the eleventh but we don't know why it affected you and why you carry a gun and smoke Cuban cigars."

Murdock and Mavis glared at each other, Murdock dropping his gaze first.

"Nosey cow," he muttered with a certain grudging respect.

"Murdock, we need to know. Edwin needs to know."

"All right, all right. I was in Boston working for an advertising firm; I drew cartoons and computer-generated graphics for television commercials. It was a bit tedious at times like most new jobs but I was living in a great town with a lovely lady called Daphne and we had two kids, one hers and one ours. She was a teacher and there was this school trip and somehow she managed to wangle a couple of seats for them to go too – I remember her main argument was that it was a once in a lifetime thing, how we could never afford it without the education subsidy. I was all set to go down to Florida for an interview at the Disney studios so I couldn't keep them with me, all right I could have but it wasn't convenient.' Murdock paused and took a long pull on his cigar before continuing, his voice raw with suppressed anger. 'I was sitting in the departure lounge eating a bagel and surfing the net when I saw the first tower hit. And then the news kept coming in about more planes. I tried ringing her, her parents, her sister, the school. By the time I managed to make a connection we all knew they'd been on the flight that had crashed in Washington. Seems like yesterday. I remember just dropping everything, getting in my car and driving across the states to be with her. I watched as they dug them out of the wreckage and I vowed that I'd never rest until their deaths had been avenged. Which is why when I was approached by the government to keep tabs on some colleagues with certain dubious Arab connections I agreed." He paused again, bit his under lip and then slowly relit the cigar.

"It was downhill from there. I moved back to Britain and officially started working for a national tabloid as one of their political cartoonists. Unofficially I also worked as a spy, or informer if you prefer that word. Learnt a lot of nasty tricks they don't teach you in self-defence classes and how to shoot a man's vital organs. A dead man can't give you any information, you see. And then the inner city riots started."

"We were told it all started with the refugees coming over and taking people's jobs," I stated, quoting the official line. " The men of Britain started rioting, by men I mean the young unemployable element. It all escalated and ended up with a primary school being petrol bombed. There was a gas explosion and ..."

"Five hundred and twenty-three souls perished in a burst of yellow flames and white hot metal," Mavis finished for me. "And then the women rose up and hit back, my mother included."

"And mine – she was a teacher and her best friend died in the fire. I think she caught one of the ringleaders," I sighed heavily because that was all my mother had ever told me about it.

"Do you know what they did to the ringleaders?" Murdock asked.

"No," Mavis and I both admitted.

"They were herded into an old concrete bunker, locked in and left."

"Was that all?" I asked. I'd expected a firing squad at the very least.

"It took the last one forty-two days to die. He must have survived by eating the dead or dying and drinking the water which seeped down from the grass above. I don't think anyone ever bothered to open the bunker up and take the bodies out although my colleagues told me that the smell died eventually."

Mavis and I shuddered: that was one story they hadn't included in my *History of England: The last decade, parts one to six*.

"But the New Management must have stopped you being

a spy or whatever they employed you as. I mean all the secret service cloak-and-dagger merchants were closed down, weren't they?" I asked.

"Officially yes. Unofficially they carried on under a different name and under the orders of the Attorney General and the police. After all we had no Royal to owe allegiance to."

"Where did they go?" I asked eagerly. I could still remember the old headlines: Buckingham Palace deserted, abandoned by top Royals; Royals do a bunk; Royal rats leave sinking Britain – there was even one stating that their rather old- fashioned if not downright quaint views on women had led to them being assassinated Russian style in the damp cellars of the Palace of Westminster.

"Ah well …"

"Yes?" both Mavis and I hissed.

"That would be telling."

"Spoilsport."

"Fascist pig."

"What I can tell you is that one of them had a bastard son."

"So?" I couldn't quite see why some love affair of the Royals should have anything to do with me and even less to do with the death of my late father. Mavis, on the other hand, sat back and looked like the cat that was about to overdose on clotted cream.

"It's true then?" she breathed, her eyes aglow.

"Oh yes, it's true all right." Murdock threw the smouldering remains of his cigar into the surrounding water and hunched further back into his jacket.

"What's true?" I asked.

"Rumour has it …" Mavis began.

"Lucky rumour," I quipped, only to be glared at by a very grim-faced Murdock.

"... that the Royal family wants England back."

"Why?" I asked.

"Probably because it's the only job they know," Mavis replied a trifle snidely.

"Actually they don't want it back," Murdock mused. "The only person who wants it is a mad religious fanatic who has the self-styled title 'George Windsor protector of the faith'. Unfortunately he also has the DNA certificate to prove that he is actually a direct descendant of the old guard and if they don't want the job of governing England and what's left of the Commonwealth, he does. He also wants complete control of the Church of England and his money back."

"Money?"

"The New Management confiscated all properties and titles to any assets owned by the Crown – how else do you think they managed to pay for the new railways and the hospitals?"

"And the schools," Mavis added.

"Exactly."

"And now this George person wants it back?"

"Yes."

"What's he going to do then? Raise an army and invade parliament?" I laughed.

Murdock and Mavis looked at each other and then stared at me, their eyes totally without humour. It was then that I realized finally what it all meant.

"But to do that he'd have to have an army."

"He has."

"Where?" I asked stunned.

"Scotland, under appropriately enough the banner of Montrose."

"But he'd also have to have weapons."

"He has them too. He may even, although I'm not saying he has, possess a very nasty invention of your mutual late lamented parent." Murdock got up and stamped his feet. He then stretched his whole frame, catching the first rays of the awakening sun on his face.

I sat huddled into myself as all the information slowly sank in.

"And this Warwick chap, whose side is he on?"

"Officially the side of his paymasters, the government. Unofficially he's on the side that will give him what he really wants and that's complete control of the secret services and the police."

"And that's what he's been promised by this Prince George?"

"Yes."

"So he's working to sabotage the government here and pass information to this Prince George in Scotland?"

"He's also drawing up a list of the old guard, all those who lost their old positions of power and Royal funding."

"But if he's raised an army and he leaves Scotland that will mean …"

My voice tailed off as I finally spoke the two words which I thought you only read about in textbooks, "Civil war!"

chapter nineteen

The plot thickens

"So your being here with us wasn't an accident?" Mavis asked.

"Not exactly," Murdock admitted.

"I still don't understand what this has got to do with me," I muttered.

"Warwick believes that your father told you something before he died," Murdock stated, watching me with the eyes of a benevolent hawk.

"But he didn't – he was going to but he never got around to it."

"Why?" Mavis asked.

"I don't know." I cast my mind back and tried to remember anything I'd previously missed. "I think he saw something or someone that frightened him, and he did a runner before he could let me know. Not that I'd have listened if he had."

"He didn't pass you anything?"

"Well I thought he'd left a carrier bag behind, that's why I was chasing him. But if it was in that, the police have it."

"And if the police have it so does our Mr Warwick," Mavis moaned.

"Not necessarily."

"Oh?" A light was beginning to dawn; the police in the hospital hadn't been all that keen to learn that he'd been to see me.

"Murdock, just exactly what are you doing here?"

"Let's just say that I owe someone a favour and leave it at that, shall we?" Murdock replied, his face closing down as he spoke. I had the impression it would have been easier to prize open the average clam than Murdock for any additional knowledge.

"So what do we do now?" Mavis asked.

"We collect our bags and start walking," Murdock grunted and disappeared down into the dark shadows of the boat.

Ten minutes later we were on our way. After five minutes of gentle trudging Murdock stopped abruptly and then dived behind a large elder bush. Mavis and I glanced at each other and then we heard it: a soft shuffling sound which was quickly following us along the path.

There was a snap as a twig was trodden on and the ominous click of a gun having the safety catch disengaged. Mavis and I turned and searched the grey, pink-edged light, our eyes straining into the distant rising canal mist. Something caught my eye, a movement near the ground and I knelt quickly into a crouching position.

And then I saw who it was and my heart sank.

"Oh no," I muttered despairingly.

"What is it?" Mavis hissed until she too saw the approaching menace. "Oh Hell!"

There was another click as we heard the safety catch being

re-engaged and Murdock emerged from his shrubbery, swearing mightily under his breath, wet leaves and the odd spider trailing in his wake.

"Now what do we do?" I asked.

"Quack," came the reply as Erik waddled speedily towards us.

"Erik, go back to the boat," Murdock hissed. "Now."

Erik looked from one to the other and shook his beak. Murdock gave a grunt of displeasure and marched off. Mavis and I followed reluctantly. After a few minutes Mavis stopped and clutched at her side.

"What's the matter?" I asked.

"Stitch. It will go in a minute. You go on ahead – if our glorious leader sees that we're flagging behind he'll probably shoot us."

"Right … er … are you sure?"

"Sure I'm sure, I just need a bit of a breather. I'll catch you up."

Shrugging my backpack into a more comfortable position I set off to follow Murdock.

I was just wondering whether I ought to request a comfort stop so that Mavis could catch up when she appeared beside me, red in the face and dripping perspiration.

"Are you sure you're all right," I asked again, this time really concerned.

"Yes."

We travelled on foot for another hour until we came to a road which ran alongside the canal. Murdock clambered over a roughly hewn stile, and pausing to check that all was clear, beckoned us to follow him.

The road ran off into the distance between tall windblown ditches and grey skeletal trees. The wind moaned around us and cobwebs sparkled and glittered from the tall white heads of cow parsley growing from the shelter of a dry ditch, which edged the road in a rich hump of verdant greens.

Finally we reached a gate leading to what looked like a collection of old abandoned farm buildings. Murdock pushed it open and left it tied back to the hedge with a piece of blue nylon rope which was looped around the rusting gate catch. Mavis and I exchanged a questioning look. The rope was very new.

The farm as we approached looked in an even more dilapidated state than it had from the road. Supporting end walls leant uncomfortably away from each other, the uneven sides blackened and charred, bricks and mortar missing from gaps where the window frames ought to have been. Most of the roof had caved in and the ground was littered with old slates and oddly twisted bits of wood.

Murdock began moving large sheets of corrugated iron from where they were leaning drunkenly against the wall and to my astonishment revealed a small squat grey van, covered in dust and grime. Shoving the last piece of camouflage to the ground he began to fumble around under the vehicle. Mavis and I drew nearer and watched as he produced a set of keys from the area behind the wheel trim.

Hastily we piled into the back and Murdock started the engine. To our mutual surprise it turned over almost immediately and within minutes we were bumping and grinding our way down the single-track road we had previously been walking up.

"There's a blanket on the floor. Get as far down as you can and pull it over you," Murdock ordered as he negotiated a large irregular pothole.

Mavis and I crouched in our increasingly uncomfortable positions until we couldn't feel our hands or feet. Something moved next to me.

"Mavis?" I whispered.

"What?"

"Did you just try to …?"

"What?"

"Er …"

My voice tailed off as the pressure on the zip of my jeans stopped.

"Nothing. It was nothing." I replied. The soft moving weight had now reached my stomach and a pair of raisin black eyes stared hopefully up at me. It was Erik and he looked hungry.

"You brought that bloody duck," I hissed at her.

"Um …"

"Murdock will probably blow a gasket and then …" I met Erik's steely gaze with my own.

"Let's just hope he can't get any sage and onion."

I was just beginning to wonder who would make a puddle first, Erik or myself, when the van stopped and Murdock opened the driver's door. Someone was waiting for us in the gloom of an old railway bridge.

"Well, I got him, now don't ask me for anything else – we barely got out in time as it was," we heard Murdock say to the silent figure.

The back door was flung open and the blanket was cast aside. Looking up I saw the person Murdock had been talking to and my heart did a sudden shaky cartwheel. Smiling down at me was Clarris Sharpe. Erik emerged from the discarded folds of wool and uttered a loud quack of disapproval.

"And what the hell is that?" Clarris asked, pointing at Erik with a perfectly manicured finger.

Murdock, Mavis and I looked towards the offending creature.

"Er, he's our … er … security officer," I replied, extracting myself from the inside of the van. "And he's hungry," I added helpfully.

"That bloody duck is always hungry," Murdock growled. "And so come to that am I."

"Follow me," Clarris ordered in the sort of voice she usually reserved for very junior members and civil servants.

She led the way across the road adjoining the bridge and passed through a low wooden doorway. We slunk in single file down a urine scented alley and finally entered a narrow hallway which had been built into the side of an end terraced house. We waited as she quietly shut the back door and then opened another, leading into a brightly decorated but sparsely furnished kitchen.

The figure of a man was bent over pots and pans, which hissed and spluttered upon an old-fashioned Aga and as we entered he turned, and seeing the look of astonishment on my face, grinned broadly.

"Pete!" I exclaimed. "What are you doing here – I thought you'd retired!"

"Not exactly retired," he laughed, wiping his hands on a cloth hanging from a rail running around the front of the cooking range. "Just a different line of business. Take a seat, it's almost ready."

"And after we've eaten," Clarris informed me with a scowl, "you and I, Edwin, are going to have a little chat and you can explain just exactly what the bloody hell is going on!"

chapter twenty

Clarris takes charge

After a meal of beef stew and dumplings washed down with several bottles of very good wine, Clarris sat back in her chair, folded her arms and stared at me. One by one the conversations around the table ceased until the only thing to be heard was the gentle ticking of an old wall clock and the soft whimpering grunt of Erik, stuffed to the gunnels and fast asleep near the Aga in an old biscuit tin full of shredded newspaper.

"So," she said softly, but with an edge to the well-groomed voice, "tell me why I have just spent the last week helping the police with their enquiries, to say nothing of being verbally abused by that shit Warwick?"

"Er ..." I glanced at Mavis, who was studiously avoiding me, and shuffled uneasily in my seat. "I ... um?"

"I really think you'd better come up with more than 'I um'," Clarris snapped. "And I'd also like to know just exactly who the accompanying piece of totty is?" Clarris's eyes glittered menacingly. I'd never really seen her like this before, in fact she was showing the first real signs of being human.

"She's my half-sister and her name is Mavis Wordsworth and before you ask I never told her about the you-know-what in room 205." Clarris had the grace to blush and Mavis looked up, her eyes brim full of gleeful interest.

There was a thought-filled pause as Clarris digested the name and then as the dawn of knowledge hit she suddenly laughed. "So that's why you were seen in France?"

"And Belgium."

"You made all that up. And the photographs?"

"Doctored old ones, new backgrounds added, lethal hardware, the usual mock-ups," Mavis admitted.

"I see. In fact you lied to the teeth and have sent several members of the police force haring off to God knows where, probably costing the taxpayer a small fortune in expenses."

"Er ..." Mavis looked uncertainly at me but I was staring at Clarris in open-mouthed astonishment.

"I don't suppose you'd consider a job as my Public Relations Manager?" Clarris chuckled with a low deep-throated roar of good humour.

Mavis gave a relieved lopsided grin and suddenly the tension of the last twenty-four hours evaporated in a miasma of wine and laughter.

"Pete, do we have any brandy?" Clarris asked, pushing her empty wine glass to one side.

Pete nodded and returned with an assortment of glasses and a large dusty bottle of a deep amber-coloured liquid.

Clarris sipped hers very delicately and gave a sigh of approval.

"So Edwin, why don't you tell me exactly what has happened to you and your accomplices since you walked out of our flat one bright Friday morning?" Clarris asked, swilling the alcohol around in the bottom of the glass whilst warming it slowly with the heat from her hands.

It took several hours to explain everything, especially as every few minutes or so Murdock or Mavis would interject and either throw in bits that I hadn't known about or amend bits I thought I had. Finally, my tale told, I sat back exhausted and stretched weary limbs; my neck had all but seized up and my head was beginning to spin as the wine and brandy began to meet up and throw individual parties with the white and red corpuscles racing around my bloodstream.

Clarris had stopped smiling and was looking almost worried – another side of her personality that she'd previously kept to herself.

"So Warwick is back to his old tricks and playing tag with the young pretender," she muttered thoughtfully.

"Perhaps we could go to the President?" I observed hopefully.

"You haven't heard?"

"Heard what?" I asked, puzzled.

"The President is on the point of resigning."

"Oh." Mavis, Murdock and myself exchanged helpless glances.

"Why?" Mavis asked.

"The official reason is that she's ill."

"And the unofficial reason?" Murdock mumbled, taking another swig of brandy.

"She doesn't want a fight with Scotland. To be perfectly frank she's a peacetime leader and the thought of what will happen in the event of a clash between the Royalists who want a king back on the throne and a return to male-dominated government and the present government, isn't something she can bring herself to contemplate."

"So what will happen?" I prompted.

"Nothing, until it's too late and the whole country is on the point of civil war. Even now Warwick is currying favour from the old guard, including the more conservative members of the clergy, especially amongst those who strongly and publicly spoke against the enthronement of the first woman Archbishop. They lost their jobs remember, in fact a lot of very powerful people lost a lot of money and influence and I really don't think forgiveness is something they instil in you at the better public schools."

"So what do we do?" I rumbled gloomily.

"Do?" Clarris looked around the table, her eyes holding each person's glance until she had our total attention.

"We go to Scotland and find out exactly what Warwick has up his sleeve and why he's so anxious to get hold of whatever it is he thinks your father left in your tender little paws," Clarris announced firmly.

"And why should we do that?" I asked mutinously. Scotland, whichever way you looked at it, was not the sort of place I wanted to travel to and I certainly didn't see why I should continue on a journey which had become, to my way of thinking, a wild goose chase and an increasingly dangerous one at that.

"Because, Edwin, unless we find out what exactly it is that Warwick thinks you have, your life isn't worth diddly squat!"

"Ah," I stammered, aghast as what Clarris saw only too clearly finally hit me. Warwick didn't know that I didn't know and rather than risk letting me find out, he'd have me permanently silenced.

Clarris gave me a long hard look before pushing her chair

back and standing up. "I'll say goodnight then," she said before adding in softer tones, "Coming, Edwin?"

Mavis and Murdock exchanged a grinning glance and I went a deep purple colour.

"Er ..." I stammered uncertainly.

"Edwin, we need to talk," Clarris hissed. "In private."

"Ah," I muttered, looking up and meeting those famous kohl-enhanced eyes.

Pete muttered something about needing to check the perimeter. Mavis yawned and asked for directions to the bathroom and her allotted bed and Murdock disappeared with vague mutterings about seeing a man about a dog.

Clarris and I were finally alone in the warm aromatic kitchen and I was suddenly aware that our relationship had irreparably changed. Clarris moved her chair towards the Aga, bumping the legs against Erik's box. Erik opened one eye, gave her the look and buried his beak further down into his wing feathers.

"What are you going to do with that duck?" Clarris finally asked.

"Don't know, but as he saved my life, probably keep him as far away from Pete and a box of citrus fruits as I can."

Clarris laughed and then grew more serious. "I've missed you," she said softly.

"Oh," I replied, not sure what to say next.

There was another silence. Finally I broke it by saying in slightly bitterer tones than I'd originally intended. "I don't see why; after all you still had Mark and Harrison to fulfil your needs."

"Is that what you think?" she asked, searching my face. "That all I want from you is sex?"

"Well, isn't it?"

"No, no, it isn't."

"Sure, and that's why I share a flat with two other guys," I snapped back.

"I don't sleep with them."

"No of course not – what do you do then, play Scrabble?"

"Sometimes."

"Oh come off it Clarris, if you don't need them for a bit of physical pleasure what the hell do you use them for?"

"Harrison is, as you know, Pete's replacement and as you are now no doubt aware, Pete works for the special services and so does Harrison."

I sat and stared at her, my mouth half-open in amazement and partial disbelief.

"Harrison's your minder?" I asked.

"No he's yours, or at least he was until he was fired."

"Fired!"

"If he'd done his job properly, Toby wouldn't have got anywhere near you and all of this could have been avoided." She angrily stretched out her hands to illustrate her point and then sank back into her chair.

"And Mark? Was he my minder?"

"No, Mark is my ears and eyes." She gave a soft sigh and added. "Everyone needs a spy, someone who can keep their ear to the ground for public and private opinions. Mark fulfils that role, he's also the only person I know who can break into the central computer network without raising any alarms or leaving a trail."

"And what function do I perform?" I asked, feeling about as useful as a chocolate teapot.

"You. You do something nobody else has ever done."

"Right."

Clarris looked straight into my eyes before replying in a

voice so soft I almost missed it.

"You make me laugh."

chapter twenty-one

Five go on holiday

The sun streaming in through the half-opened window hit my eyes at about the same time as someone began to lick the edge of my shoulder.

"Get up, you lazy sod," it murmured huskily.

I mumbled something fairly rude and turned my head into my pillow.

"Oh come on Edwin, I want to see what you think?"

Something sat on the side of the bed, and brushed her lips against my buried cheek. Groggily I began to sit up and as my eyes started to focus properly, the nightmare vision of what I was seeing came into sharp focus.

"Clarris! What the bloody hell have you done to your hair?"

"Done? Oh Edwin darling, don't you like it? I think it's rather me."

Clarris got up off the bed and preened in front of the mirror hanging at a slightly rakish angle on the opposite wall. I simply stared at her, my eyeballs popping. She had cut her hair and the long glorious mane of golden brown curls that I'd fallen in lust with had been replaced by a short spiky helmet, the longest spike being about half an inch long.

"It's orange!" I squeaked. "And what the hell is that hanging from your eyebrow?"

"It's a diamond stud. All the rage with the youth of today."

"Who told you that porkie?" I snarled, discarding the bedclothes. I was rummaging around for my clothes when Clarris returned to sit cross-legged on the other side of the bed.

"I thought you'd like it – you know, a new age Clarris for the new age you."

"Well I don't, and …" I added, finding my jeans tucked under a chair, "I'm not going anywhere near you with that thing there. You haven't done anything else?" I asked suspiciously.

"Like what?"

"You know!"

"Know what?" she replied, all innocence.

"Nipple bits and … er … other … er … private places." I glared at her as my head emerged through the neck of my jumper.

"They say owners grow like their pets."

"What?"

"You – for a moment you looked just like that bloody duck!"

Clarris laughed and slowly unscrewed the ring stud from her brow.

"So is the rest all right, sir?" she asked, getting up and spinning slowly round.

I observed the new orange-haired Clarris and had to

admit that with a baggy sweatshirt, old frayed jeans and trainers she didn't look anything like her normal self, in fact she didn't look even vaguely related.

"I can honestly say that no one would recognize you as a member of the government, or for that matter a member of the human race!" I acidly remarked. Clarris chuckled and handed me a sock.

Looking down on her, I suddenly saw her as a lot younger; gone were the carefully airbrushed and manicured looks and in their place was a somewhat smaller, saucer-eyed pixie.

"You know, with the stud gone I could almost fancy you," I said in a fairly husky manner as a certain part of my anatomy rose to the occasion.

"Really?" Clarris murmured, moving closer.

"Really," I whispered, kissing her.

Later we lay together side by side in a state of undress, as my mother would have said, and stared at the cracks in the ceiling.

"Clarris?"

"Mm."

"I think I love you."

"That's nice."

"Thing is ..."

"What?"

"I don't want to go back to what we had before."

"Oh."

"I don't want to share you."

"Oh goodie, I love it when you get all uppity and dominant."

"Clarris, I'm serious. I want you without anybody else and I want ..."

"Yes?"

"I want a job." There I'd said it; finally the worm had turned. There was complete silence as this new state of affairs was turned over in the Clarris brain.

"OK."

"What?" I sat up and looked down on her as she lay, eyes closed, beside me.

"I said OK." Clarris opened both eyes and fixed me with a steely blue look. "I'll sort something out when we get back to London, that is if I still have a job to go back to myself."

"Maybe we don't have to go back?" I remarked as I started to dress for the second time that day.

"And what do you suggest we do?" she asked, wriggling back into her jeans.

"Well we could run a barge or a pub or something?"

"Would you really like that?" Clarris asked, searching my face as if she was seeing it for the first time.

"Yes," I stated, pulling on my trainers, "I really think I would. In fact I know I would and I'd be good at it."

There was a tentative knock on the door and Pete shouted through the keyhole that we needed to get going.

"Clarris?"

"We'll sort it all out, I promise." Clarris smiled and stroked the flesh behind my ear with a long finger. "But just at the moment we need to get going or we'll miss the coach."

"What coach?" I asked, following her from the room and descending the stairs two at a time.

"The coach Pete and I have booked with the company that will, if all goes well, get us to our next port of call before tomorrow night and before Warwick twigs that I've gone AWOL."

"And where's that?"

"The Isle of Man."

I stopped at the bottom of the stairs and thoughtfully asked, while my mind began to look at the ramifications of leaving England.

"But they don't let anyone in without a passport and a holiday visa?"

"I know, Pete's had it all sorted: false passports, false records and a friend of his with a small, fast boat ready and waiting in a quiet, seldom used and mostly ignored landing stage."

"You really do think of everything," I said admiringly.

"No, I do," Pete chuckled as he passed us in the hall on his way to the back door.

"Come on you two, everyone else is ready and waiting and the coach will only stop for two minutes."

I hurried off to the downstairs toilet and a few minutes later joined my fellow travelling companions in the alley behind the house. I arrived to find Murdock having a very heated conversation with Mavis over a brown cardboard box that Mavis was hugging to herself.

"I'm not leaving him behind," Mavis mouthed.

"We can't take a duck on a coach!" Murdock shouted back.

Mavis glared belligerently up at him and stuck out her chin.

"I can."

"No, you ruddy well can't." Murdock suddenly realized I was there and grabbed me before I could escape. "Edwin, you're a sensible lad, you tell her."

I shuffled uneasily as both of them fixed me with equally

forceful eyes and Erik peered at me from over the top of the corrugated cardboard rim.

"Well …" I mumbled awkwardly, "it would be difficult but on the other hand he did save our lives. Sort of …."

"Fat lot of good you are!" Murdock bellowed.

"What's up?" Clarris asked, arriving just as it looked as if Murdock was ready to forcibly remove the box from Mavis's arms.

"Mavis says we can't leave that bloody duck here!" Murdock exploded.

"Well, what do you think Edwin?" Clarris asked.

"Me?" Since when did I start making decisions, I helplessly thought, and more importantly when had I ever been allowed to make them? I was still trying to think of a compromise when Pete arrived at our side and began to chivvy us down towards the road.

We set off, Mavis clutching the box, Murdock glaring balefully and Clarris swinging her arms and grinning like a teenager. I followed feeling at least twenty years older than the lot of them with the possible exception of Pete who was looking grey and worried. His frown cleared as we reached the coach stop on the other side of the bridge and a plain blue van approaching us from the other side of the road crossed the white lines in the middle and slewed to a halt besides him.

An arm bearing a large tattoo of a bull sitting on an eagle with a telescope in its hands was thrust out of the window. Pete grabbed the box from Mavis and hurriedly handed it to the arm, which drew it into the van and then with a hiss of tyres drove off in a flurry of dust and bits of loose tarmac.

Mavis stood and watched, her mouth slack and obviously for one of the few times in her life completely lost for words.

"He's a colleague and he has a pond," Pete informed us as he handed each of us a plastic envelope containing what looked like a collection of tickets and an old worn-looking passport. I watched the vehicle until I couldn't hear it any more and silently wished Erik a good time and a long life.

A coach rumbled into sight. It was a bright peacock blue with the legend 'Tara Travel' written in gold on the side. It stopped further down the road and the side door opened with a snake-like hiss.

"Come on you lot, I haven't got all day. Sit where you like and don't use the bog, the wretched thing won't flush."

Clarris giggled and made her way to an empty window seat halfway along. I sat beside her after depositing our bags in the overhead rack. Clarris murmured something which sounded like, "Love you," and rested a spiky head on my shoulder.

I muttered something vaguely soft back and kissed the top of her head. It was with something of a jolt that I realized that we had never really been alone like this before. I also realised that I was now making decisions and that people were finally taking notice of what I said. I wasn't sure what we would find at the end of our journey but whatever it was the one thing I was now really certain of was that there really was no turning back.

chapter twenty-two

On the buses

We bounced and rumbled our way towards Coventry. Every so often we'd stop and pull in at a gaily painted stop and pick up a few more passengers. Our driver would grunt at them, cross a few more lines off his list and then inform them about the non-existent state of the facilities.

After about half an hour we found ourselves rattling along a motorway, the coach swaying happily as it picked up speed and finally managed top gear. Our driver hung over the steering wheel and hummed tunelessly to the music pulsing from the radio beside him. The sun winked and blinked at me from the gaps in the high fence lining the hard shoulder and I began to succumb to the soporific effect of the warmth and the softly seductive scent of Clarris's shoulder.

With a lurch and a rumble the coach turned away from the stream of fast moving lorries, vans and coaches and began to climb up towards a large wood-lined roundabout. With a groan of brakes and a hiss of gears we stop-started our way across and then travelled a mile or so down a newly surfaced road. Other identically painted coaches began to appear in front and behind us as we passed a blue and white checkpoint complete with gold striped barrier and a portly guard rapidly speaking into a small mobile phone whilst making various hand signals, some of them very rude, to the approaching drivers.

Our own driver slewed to a halt in front of a large pole bearing a black and red number twenty-nine and with a flourish opened the door and began to assist the elderly couple at the front through it, despite their protestations and high pitched squeaks that they were really "All right thank you".

Clarris and I collected our things and followed the stream of humanity into the large hangar-like building in front of us. Somewhere above our heads an adenoidal voice of indeterminate sex advised all drivers to collect their papers and go to the briefing room. The voice was cut off in mid-whine and was replaced by someone who sounded very much like my old primary school headmistress.

"Would all passengers please see their tour representatives immediately and await embarkation at their correctly numbered stop. Please ensure that all baggage has been marked with the correct information by affixing the labels provided by the company. Tea, coffee and sandwiches are available from the café and would all parents please ensure that their children use the toilet facilities provided, before embarkation." There was a slight pause followed by a terse "Thank you".

Clarris and I looked at each other just as Pete approached, grinning and bearing a large plastic-wrapped roll with something pink hanging from it.

"Before you ask I've seen the label and it's supposed to

be ham. I'm just not sure if it was dead before they stuck it in," Pete informed us, prodding the round of doughy bread with a finger.

"I think I'll stick to tuna," I grunted, watching in fascination as Pete took his first bite.

"Or maybe cheese," I added as the roll was lobbed expertly towards a waiting bin.

"Knew I should have stuck with the raspberry Danish," Pete grunted, wiping his mouth with the back of his hand. "I don't suppose either of you have seen Murdock and young Mavis?" Clarris and I shook our heads.

It was as we bumbled off towards the central café area that I realized I hadn't actually seen either of them since we had boarded the coach.

"Is it me?" Clarris asked rather hesitantly as we queued up to pay, clutching our sandwiches and plastic beakers of coffee.

"What?" I asked, fumbling in my pockets for some money.

"The reason Mavis has been avoiding you."

"Why would she do that?" I asked, handing over a couple of coins.

"You tell me," Clarris replied.

At that moment another announcement was uttered over the airwaves, this time accompanied by a musical bong.

"All feeder coaches have now arrived. Would all passengers please go to their respective embarkation points. All drivers to their stations."

"Feeder coaches?" I grinned at Clarris who smiled back.

There was an indistinct ping and the first voice was back.

"Would Mr Arnold Wayne Harris travelling from Bromsgrove to Poland please go to the information desk where he may collect his medication? Thank you."

Clarris choked on a bit of tomato and it was as I was patting her on the back that a soft voice whispered in my ear, "Pity you don't have a sharp instrument on you."

"Mavis?" I turned to find her standing behind me and scowling.

"Have you seen this?" Mavis demanded, waving one of the more lurid daily tabloids at me.

"Seen what?" I asked, giving the back a final slap. Clarris, red-faced and shaking, sat down on a nearby plastic chair and tried to get her breath back.

"Page ten, bottom paragraph under the title 'Postman bites dog', and 'Three legged Elvis seen in Stoke Newington'."

I prised open the pages and finally found the piece I was supposed to be looking for. At first I couldn't quite believe what I'd read and so I read it again. It didn't get any better.

> Clarris Sharpe, that well known exponent of the uplift bra and stocking-top glimpses has been cautioned by police following her outspoken condemnation of her ex-lover, the mad arsonist Edwin Snipe. The fracas happened outside the home of Edwin's father. William Snipe and a male friend are now undergoing treatment at St Augustine's hospital. Ms Sharpe will also be questioned about her behaviour at a dinner held in honour of the Spanish ambassador at which she poured half a bottle of Rioja over a senior civil servant's head. Ms Sharpe was unavailable for comment yesterday although a close friend has told us that she has had a few medical problems recently and that they are worried about the amount of drink and drugs being consumed by the Clarris menagerie.

"We need to talk," Clarris managed to stutter between gasps for breath.

"Later," I hissed back, folding the paper and dumping it

in the nearest bin.

"Well?" Mavis asked, looking from me to Clarris and back again.

"What?" I snarled.

"What are you going to do about it?" Mavis replied, clearly puzzled.

"Nothing. For the moment." I looked down on Clarris whose white face stared back at me. "We need to get on our coach and then after I've had something to eat, I'll sort something out. What I don't need to do, is to have every member of the press and security crawling out of the woodwork before we get to where we are going and find out what it is that I don't know but everyone else thinks I do. And may I also remind you, sister dearest, that it isn't your head everyone wants but mine."

It was at that opportune moment that Pete returned, clutching the ends of a mangled pastry and began to shepherd us to our waiting coach. We boarded our new mode of transport, which looked exactly like the previous one, and found our allotted seats. The driver entered last and began to move towards us, counting heads.

"Anybody seen Mr and Mrs Scavin?" he asked. There was a brief silence broken by the arrival of a middle-aged couple clutching a selection of weathered plastic bags.

"You're late," the driver growled at them as they settled into their seats.

"Sorry," Mr Scavin muttered, his eyes glinting weakly from behind thick-rimmed bi-focals.

The head counting began again until the driver finally went back to his seat and after checking the rear view mirrors and doors to his satisfaction turned on the engine.

"My name is Bob," boomed a voice from the ceiling, "and

I am your driver and tour guide for the length of your holiday in the Isle of Man." There was a pause as something was adjusted on the panel in front of him.

"Today we will be travelling to Heysham and from there by ferry to the Isle of Man. The ferry will take approximately three hours to reach the island and you may purchase food and drink on board if you wish, as dinner is not provided by the hotel on the first night of your arrival as specified on page thirteen of your holiday brochure."

There was a screech of brakes as we did a broad, arcing sweep before leaving the coach depot and the beaming guard.

"There are tea and coffee-making facilities at the back of the coach and I will be handing out vouchers later on today."

The coach began to pick up speed and fairly raced towards the sliproad onto the M6 motorway.

"Meals are provided by the hotel and will be of a buffet variety, as much as you can eat and it's normally bloody good so if you're on one of them stupid diets, forget it."

There was a slight hiatus as our coach waited its turn before joining the string of traffic on the motorway.

"Tomorrow I'll go through our tour itinerary and take the money off you for the optional excursions including the Gaiety Theatre tour, play and supper, the Steam and Electric Railway mystery tour and the basking shark and seal boat trip. Details of which you will find on the front noticeboard near reception."

A coach suddenly zipped past us, the driver waving frantically to Bob as he passed.

"Bloody George," Bob muttered, speeding up. "Bugger used to race bleedin' rally cars till they banned them for being too friggin' dangerous, now he races buses."

There was a general tut, tut from our fellow passengers, some of it directed towards our driver's vocabulary, rather than on the re-run of 'Wacky Races'. Our coach swayed and began to catch the other coach up. A Tesco lorry in front of us hastily indicated and pulled into the slow lane only just in time. Up ahead a stream of vehicles also headed off to the side. A coach travelling the other way flashed its headlights and Bob and George slowed down until a more sedate and legal pace had been achieved. Two coaches following behind also slowed and we rumbled on to the sudden sounds of an old recording of 'Convoy', which Bob was now releasing over the intercom. When the singer had reached the bit about bears on the bumper we finally spotted the police car squatting on a mound of earth and tarmac beside the motorway. The coaches passed the clearly disgruntled constabulary in slow formation with each driver smartly saluting the garishly decorated vehicle.

There was a titter of sound from Murdock. Clarris watched round-eyed and then with a visible sigh of relief settled back further into her seat.

"Go on, ask her," Mavis hissed from behind me.

"I'll ask when we get on the ferry," I replied, finally opening my packet of tuna sandwiches. "And now I want to eat my lunch in peace."

Clarris gave me an odd look and began to unwrap her own vacuum-sealed pack. Mavis gave a loud huff of disappointment and moodily kicked the back of my seat. The elderly couple in front turned to stare at her in tandem as if she were some sort of delinquent child and then resumed their lunch. I had goggled when they carefully unfolded identical gingham napkins and then had produced a china plate, cup and various stainless steel utensils, but the mind had positively boggled, turned a somersault and then gone off in disgust when the miniature picnic hamper had come out. Somehow the combination of a coach holiday, the Isle of Man, cold chicken, foie gras and half-bottle of champagne didn't exactly gel.

But then again it takes all sorts. On the one hand we had the Formby-Smythes (with an 'e'); he wore a three-piece suit with cravat and matching handkerchief, its ironed triangular corner poking rakishly from his top breast pocket, his wife the epitome of elderly purple-haired chic in a light linen suit with matching accessories, and then you had the Boltons who were visiting the wife's relatives, as Mr Bolton was at pains to inform anyone who came within shouting distance. The Boltons made the term 'lowest common denominator' and then downgraded it. Clarris folded herself further into her seat when they passed and even Mavis, who was generally speaking the doyenne of the oppressed, held her tongue. They had four ghastly children, one of whom was in nappies and seemed to be constantly crying, the other three sat at the back of the coach and either glazed out of the window or fought. Their parents took no notice whatsoever and continued to belch and fart their way through six large cans of lager and a bag of pickled eggs.

The entrance to the ferry terminal couldn't come quick enough.

We hurriedly disembarked, hastening en masse from the sounds, smells and gloom of the Boltons and hastily produced our passports, looking behind all the while to see if they were following. The large navy and white-clad suit on passport control gave me a somewhat suspicious glance before she espied what it was that Clarris and I were trying to avoid. Then there was an intake of breath and in tones of deep gloom she announced, “Sorry mate, but you ain’t coming on board, not after the last time.”

I goggled up at her in stunned disbelief. What the hell was she on about – what last time?

chapter twenty-three

All aboard the *Skylark*

The lady in the suit looked down from her immense and vastly superior size and with the flick of a hairy tattoo-encrusted hand, called in the reinforcements. Four men in black and luminous yellow jackets moved in, each wearing identical scowls. A woman emerged from behind a grey, moss covered pillar and watched, hugging a large metal clipboard to her chest.

I gulped and looked from one to the other. It was then that I realized they weren't staring at me but at something or someone behind Clarris. Mavis coughed beside me and the suit looked down.

"What? Oh you can go. I want a word or two with laddo here."

There was the sound of air being expelled from a small aperture and Clarris, Mavis, Murdock, Pete and myself walked briskly away covering our mouths and noses. At last in the relative safety and sweeter air of the holding area, we turned to watch the human drama being played out behind us.

Mr Bolton was being frogmarched towards a waiting van marked 'Security' and Mrs Bolton and the children were huddled in a corner looking a trifle apprehensive. The large suit, after consulting a handheld radio, grinned at them all before pointing skywards. There was a brief whistling noise and then a deep male voice boomed across the terminal.

"Would all passengers for the Isle of Man please move to Gate 4? This does not include you, Mr Wayne Bolton, as an exclusion order accepted and authorized by the Manx courts is still in effect and does not become invalid until the year two thousand and eighty four, by which time I will no longer be captain of this vessel and you will be somebody else's problem."

There was a short, silence-filled pause as everyone turned to stare at Mr Bolton, who was now a brilliant shade of red.

"What do you mean – excluded?" he bellowed.

The woman with the list whispered something into the ear of the suit, who grinned back at Mr Bolton in the time-honoured way of all law enforcement officers who regularly trained at some martial arts club but never had anyone to practice on.

"The original order was set up at the request of a Mrs Shimmin and countersigned by two police officers and the owner of the Ballanard Hotel."

"What?" Mr Bolton had turned in fury towards his wife who was now a whiter shade of pale and had started to walk backwards towards the railway entrance.

"Your friggin' mother never liked me," he screamed.

The woman with the clipboard said something to Mrs Bolton who turned towards her and briefly nodded; we watched with great interest as she marched back to the passport controller clutching her brood of now strangely quiet offspring. The suit looked at her outstretched passport and curtly nodded her through the thin gap in the white-painted chains, which dangled like half-forgotten Christmas decorations around the entrance to the car and passenger ramps. Beyond them the *Corkhill Pride*, a huge mostly white vessel, gently bobbed in the incoming tide. It had a short stubby end into which various vehicles were being escorted, after being sprayed with some sort of liquid and then checked with long poles to which were attached a series of mirrors.

"Where the hell are you going?" Mr Bolton roared.

"Mother's," was the short reply.

Mr Bolton, now trembling with rage, was escorted past the security van and on towards a small door marked 'Interrogation Rooms' and Mrs Bolton continued on her way to Gate 4.

I watched her go and then grinned down at Clarris who was still clutching my hand in a vice-like grip.

"I thought he was going to stop us," she muttered nervously. "I actually felt like a criminal."

"And how did that feel?" I asked, intrigued. After all, to a politician, lying, cheating and misappropriating the odd thousand or so must have been all in a day's work.

"Oddly horrible," she whispered back.

"If you think she was bad, you wait until you get to the Department of Immigration Control in the Island," Murdock advised darkly as he began to move towards the skulking vessel.

"What – you haven't been here before, have you?" I asked.

"Yep, used to come over regular to write up the reports for the TT, and do the cartoons for the local rag. Good crack it was, I can tell you."

"So when was the last one you did?" Mavis enquired, as

we began to climb up the stairs to the wooden bridge suspended by ropes and chains between the dockside and the boat.

"Last June." Murdock chuckled at the look on our faces. "Which means that if your master plan for getting off should unfortunately fail, I know a man who might be able to help."

Pete and Clarris exchanged startled looks and then marched purposely across the gangplank. Murdock watched them go, a dawning suspicion growing in his brain.

"They do have a plan, don't they?" he asked in dark undertones as we followed.

I shrugged. "How the hell should I know? I'm just a political pet."

"What's he on about now?" Murdock whispered to Mavis, who was looking suitably chagrined.

"Er ... nothing ... just something I may have said in the heat of the moment."

Mavis almost ran after me as I walked quickly towards the sign saying 'Gents'. Clarris and Pete were huddled together in the lee of a stairwell as I passed.

"Meet me in Woodford's Brasserie," Clarris hissed as I opened the door to sanctuary.

"All right," I muttered as I hurried inside, desperate for the facilities. The door clanged shut behind me and I stumbled off towards the end cubicle.

Later, after I'd left the deodorant-scented confines of the toilets and managed to get lost three or four times, once landing up outside the drivers' restaurant where beefy Neanderthals stared at me over the top of their all day breakfasts, I finally stood outside a white glossy door with the legend 'Woodfords Brasserie' painted in black and gold over both sides of the opening.

A smartly dressed waiter ushered me in and I hurried off towards my fellow travellers, already comfortably seated and collectively drooling over an embossed menu complete with a red silk tassel. Other diners either bent to their respective troughs of excellence or conversed in hushed whispers as they sheltered from the world outside in their individual black velvet upholstered booths.

Clarris moved up as I sat down in the one remaining space, and handed me the menu. I nearly had apoplexy at the prices, which were, considering the ingredients unbelievably reasonable. Salivating with all the earnestness of one of Pavlov's dogs I ran my eyes down the list. There were twenty-two starters alone and three pages of main courses. I didn't dare look at the sweets in case I had a seizure of some kind. Those tuna sandwiches seemed an awful long time ago.

Finally, as the waiter hovered like a large white and blue dragonfly I whittled my choices down to four starters and six main courses.

"Er, um …" I dribbled, 'I'll have the homemade chicken liver pate with the red onion marma … No, hang on, I'll have the … Murdock, what the hell are queenies?"

"Local scallops – very small and juicy," the sage replied. "For God's sake hurry up Edwin, I'm starving."

"I'll have the queenies and avocado with Pernod and cream."

"Is Sir sure?"

"Why, are they off?" I asked anxiously.

"He'll have the Queenies," Pete stated very firmly. "Come on Eddie, you only have one choice left and the rest of us would like to eat."

"Today," Mavis muttered.

"Um, I'll have the Duck with ..." A vision of Erik gunning for the man in the brown suit suddenly swam in front of me. "No, better make that the fillet steak with the blue cheese sauce."

"Salad or a selection of vegetables?"

"Er, vegetables. Are there any chips?"

"There are always chips," our waiting attendant intoned in accents of deep disapproval before collecting our menus and departing, his place instantly taken by a gentleman in a dark suit and red bow tie.

"Would you like to see the wine list?" he asked, brandishing a large gold-embossed file.

It took us ten minutes of earnest discussion to settle on two bottles of Fleurie and one of Meursault. Murdock and Clarris had opted for the pan-fried red mullet.

The starter arrived with the wine and we began the dissection. Peace reigned supreme as each morsel was savoured, chewed and then devoured.

"Murdock, is all the food on the Island like this?" I asked, spearing the last scallop and wiping the remains of the cream sauce up with a sliver of bread.

"No."

"Oh."

"Some of it's better."

"So what's it like?"

"What?"

"The Isle of Man."

"Probably the most beautiful place on God's earth when the sun shines and the home of two hundred and twenty-five different types of precipitation when it doesn't," Murdock replied, grinning.

"Tell us more," Mavis demanded, taking a sip of wine.

"Well it has one of the oldest governments in the world, one of the most successful business centres, a lucrative film industry and is one of the toughest places to get into that I know," Murdock replied, pouring the last of the white into his glass. "The evaporation rate in here must be very high," he muttered, waving an arm for the wine waiter who materialized with the promptness of a master magician and after a brief whispered conversation departed just as soundlessly.

"Why?" I asked.

"It all started with the foot and mouth crisis. The island was ringed with the wretched disease but as they had had no outbreaks since 1890 they took a very strong and successful stance on inspection and disinfection of anyone or anything going in or out. Then the drug wars started getting really nasty in Liverpool, Manchester and Birmingham, so a zero tolerance was introduced, unlike the UK which legalized cannabis and ecstasy."

"Zero tolerance, like in New York?" Mavis asked.

"Sort of – what they actually did was escort anyone caught in possession of any non-prescription drugs to the ferry terminal, where they pressed a single ticket into their hot sweaty little paws and told them to bugger off out of it."

"Wasn't that a bit harsh?" Clarris muttered as our empty bread-wiped plates were whisked out of sight.

"No, not really. I'd say it was all a matter of choice; stay and live in relative peace but accept the rules of the majority or leave."

"Seems fair enough to me," Pete agreed.

"And what about the riots and the New Management?" I asked.

"Never happened – the Island battened down the hatches,

closed ranks and like a large supertanker sat out at sea and waited for the storm to die down. Which it eventually did," Murdock stated matter-of-factly as our main courses arrived.

"The Island was asked to join the Confederation of Matriarchal Countries," Clarris said before darkly adding. "It declined."

"Why?" I asked.

"Why not?" Murdock growled. "Why change something which has happily worked for two thousand years? The island was self-sufficient in food, had good supplies of power with the newly erected wind and water farms and a healthy economy."

"So what did they do?" I asked, cutting into my steak.

"Stuck two fingers up in the air and waited for the main chance. After all, where else can you get the sort of organically raised food you are now devouring?"

"They get my vote," Mavis muttered, her mouth full of corn-fed, sage-stuffed chicken.

"They could have joined us; it would have made them safer," Clarris snapped.

"Against what? Some lawless bunch of pontificating feminists, who inherited a crap infrastructure and an education system on its last illiterate legs? Bloody English always think they know better than anyone else and then bury their collective heads in the sand over their own self-inflicted problems. Mainly due to mass incompetence," Murdock snarled back, waving his fork in the air like a pike.

"Bloody English – who the hell do you think you are?" Clarris hissed back.

There was a short silence while they tried to out-stare

each other. Clarris looked away first and violently speared a piece of fish, stabbing loudly at the white glaze of her gold-edged plate.

"Manx. That's what I am. And proud of it," Murdock replied with a glint in his eye.

"Manx!" Mavis goggled.

"Then tell me why, my little three-legged anarchist, if it was all so bloody perfect, did you leave?" Clarris asked.

"Because ..." Murdock suddenly looked a trifle sheepish. "I was asked to."

There was a stunned silence, broken by Mavis who hoarsely whispered the one word we all wanted to ask.

"Why?"

"I'm a cartoonist and our politicians have many stirring and admirable qualities, but unfortunately a sense of humour isn't one of them."

"Oh come on, it couldn't have been that bad," I stated, nibbling on a green bean.

"Couldn't it?" Clarris muttered, remembering the handyman cartoon with a shudder.

"Well, I thought depicting the Head of the Opposition as a dopey elderly caveman having trouble with a sabre-toothed tiger which bore a passing resemblance to the Minister for Health was a master stroke. Unfortunately it came the week after the one depicting the Chief Minister and the shared brain cell in the goldfish bowl."

"They do allow me back every year for the TT and to see my family, and I can always retire there but ..."

"It's difficult going back?" Clarris asked knowingly.

"Yes. Besides which I love the life on a barge. That nomadic existence of moving from pub to pub, and the Isle of Man has many things but no canals. I guess I'll think about it when I'm too old and weak to open a lock gate on my own. And now, if everyone has finished …" he looked around the table, his eyes closely resembling that of our recently removed security officer just before he leapt for the last bread roll. "Let's get the menu back, I can strongly recommend the bread and butter pudding and the treacle sponge."

chapter twenty-four
The Island

Stuffed to the gunnels with food and drink, Murdock had ordered special coffees all round. I hung over the rails and watched the grey-washed sea welling and boiling as the *Corkhill Pride* raced across its darkening surface.

Down on the dockside the bobbing boat had reminded me of an old pet, a white highland terrier we had once owned, straining at the end of his leash before his evening run. Now as the steam packet boat scurried past the old abandoned gas rigs, I was reminded of Old Scruffy Dog once again; I just hoped this one didn't take quite as many comfort stops as old Scruff had done. I was remembering the time I'd taken him out for a walk with my mother; I must have been about six, when he'd been stalked for nearly the entire length of our suburban road by a young collie that obviously thought he was a sheep. Scruff had taken umbrage at being stalked and had bared his fangs and woofed in a very threatening manner. It had taken the combined strength of both my mother and myself to stop him hurling himself across the road and into the path of an articulated lorry carrying several years' supply of cat food.

A gentle breeze blew drunkenly into one ear, tinged with the subtle aroma of garlic and Grand Marnier. "Penny for them?" it asked, leaning against me.

"Just thinking about an old friend," I replied. The soft shape of a tipsy Clarris stiffened somewhat. "Anyone I know?" she asked, her voice far less friendly.

"Not unless you can converse with the dead."

She blinked up at me. "We had a sort of dog, looked like a sheep with legs but had the soul of the average timber wolf, did everything but my maths homework," I mused, staring out at a gull gamely battling the elements and flying parallel with the boat.

"Edwin?"

"Ummm ..."

"What is that thing?"

"What thing, Pumpkin," I replied, nibbling at her ear lobe like a tentative over-sexed budgie. For a fleeting moment I wondered if there were any cabins available.

"That slug sitting between your nose and upper lip, the hairy crossbreed with attitude."

I drew back, hurt to the core.

"Clarris!"

"I mean – it's not deliberate, is it? Because with the simple application of a reasonably sharp razor ..." The question hung between us, our relationship poised on a knife-edge.

"I like it, it adds ..." Somewhere in my short vocabulary there must be a word which would suit the occasion. "... Character."

There was a snort below me as Clarris gurgled into my chest, the feathery curling hair on the top of her shorn head tickling my chin.

"Character." There was another giggle, quickly smothered.

"And I'm not getting rid of it. You take all of me with the moustache or you can bugger off."

"Oh." There was a short pause.

"Well in that case …"

"Yes?"

"I'll get used to it."

I bent to nibble the ear some more.

"Edwin, Honey bun."

"Ummm."

"That bit in the paper – it wasn't exactly the truth."

"Which bit, in what paper?"

"The paper Mavis found."

"Ahh …"

"You see, your father and I staged the fight when we saw this photographer trying to hide behind his wheelie bin. You see, I had to see him – I was desperate to find you. Especially when Pete and I got to the hospital to smuggle you out and you'd already gone."

"You really came to rescue me?"

"Well, yes. I also wanted to strangle you with my bare hands for getting me involved with that shit Warwick."

I sighed; that was more like the old Clarris.

"Then we saw the photographer lurking around outside, after I'd had a heart to heart with Bill and Ben over a pot of tea and some herbal biscuits."

"Herbal biscuits?" Dad wouldn't have, would he? Not his special blend of wacky backy and ginseng. Actually, yes he would. I swallowed and wondered what else they'd talked about and if there was a tape.

"So we set up this fight and then to make it look like I'd

really gone a little bonkers, I tipped wine over that fat smarmy git's head. Which, by the way, I enjoyed and given half a chance I'd do it again."

There was something going on here that I wasn't being told but I could work on it later when we reached our hotel.

"And then you tracked me down and here you are," I added blithely.

"Yes."

Oh yes, something was definitely going on in the Clarris brain box, something so awesomely devious that even the great Machiavelli himself would be taking notes. Still it could wait until after I'd managed to get to the land of the single malt and to the one person who would know what it was that had got my recently deceased sperm donor killed. And then … and then I would, as Fagin would say 'be reviewing the situation; I may even have to think it out again'.

"Mavis doesn't like me very much, does she?" Clarris asked, pouting slightly.

"Mavis is a journalist, she doesn't like anyone," I replied, attempting to smooth the ruffled feathers.

"Is she really your sister?"

"Yes."

"Oh."

"And before you ask, I really think she's in this thing with me simply to track down our father's killer."

"Good." Clarris expelled air through her nose in a relieved sort of way.

"Of course the possibility of an exclusive is also a major factor."

"What! Edwin, have you finally lost the plot? Have you forgotten the golden rule …"

"The mantra instilled in me with my morning coffee and evening gin. Never talk to …"

"The guttersnipes of the press!"

"But she's …"

"What?" I could tell from the barely repressed snarl, that the old Clarris was back, complete with frown and darkly knitted brow.

"Family." There was a snort of rage and I neatly stepped sideways, a move which the leading light of the Ballet Rambert would have been hard pushed to achieve, thus avoiding being punched in the small intestine.

"Family!"

"She's my sister."

"Half sister."

"I like her."

"She's a parasite, a semi literate tick, a …"

"Talking about me again, eh?" asked a barbed voice behind me.

"Well …" I stopped. Stronger men than I would have handed in the towel at this point and run screaming for the hills. The only thing stopping me was the bloodlust glinting from the eyes of the two women I had grown to love most in the world, and the small fact that everyone would think it was my fault. They always did.

"Look," I shouted pointing across the shimmering waters as a gold ribbed sun began to sink slowly behind the low bank of rose-pink clouds, hugging the far horizon.

"What?" they both asked, still squaring up like a couple of bantamweights on steroids.

"Land."

They stopped and turned towards the rim of unmistakable hills and lights, blinking and winking across the intervening foam.

"Ah, home," breathed a voice as Murdock materialized at my side, a large evil-smelling cigar clenched between his lips. "I can almost smell the kippers and the land reclamation site from here."

As the grey and purple landmass drew ever closer I breathed a sigh of relief; war had been averted, but, as Murdock whispered in my ear, only just.

chapter twenty-five

But no one expects the Spanish Inquisition

Tired but still happy from the amount of alcohol swilling around in my bloodstream, I girded my loins and prepared to battle my way through Security. Murdock had warned us all to tell the truth where possible and giggle drunkenly when not. What he hadn't told us was that before entering the hallowed rocks and halls of the Isle of Man we'd have to face the modern equivalent of the Spanish Inquisition in separate booths.

There were two people in mine, one a rather attractive brunette in a stunningly filled uniform and a short squat chap of indeterminate age who looked like a particularly hacked-off garden gnome who'd been left out in the rain for so long that someone had swiped his fishing rod

"Right," said the gnome, consulting a list on his clipboard. "Now, who would you be?"

"Er …"

"Your name?"

"Oh, right. It's …" Bloody hell – I'd forgotten.

The gnome edged nearer and then backed off as the aroma of wine and garlic reached his nostrils.

"Passport?"

I rummaged in my pockets and produced one rather bent and soggy passport. This was studied with careful nonchalance and then dumped unceremoniously on the small formica-topped table beside him.

"Pockets. Empty. Now," he bellowed as if speaking to an idiot child.

I obliged, discovering a half-eaten packet of cheese and onion crisps, a small ball of string and a quantity of paper handkerchiefs in varying states of disintegration.

"They're Erik's," I said helpfully, pointing at the crisps.

"Erik?"

"He's a duck," I added.

"A duck?" the gnome repeated, waggling his eyebrows at the brunette.

"For security."

"You trying to be funny, lad?" the gnome asked, totally unamused.

"Er no, just thought you'd like to know," I muttered, going a faint puce.

"Beryl, the metal detector – but first …" There was a short dramatic pause. "I'll have those disgusting metal objects you have embedded in your skin on this tray or you can go back to the boat."

They watched as I gingerly tried to remove the offending body jewellery. Luckily the brunette produced something which could have been a pair of pliers and removed the ring from my eyebrow without causing it to bleed too much.

"Any others you'd like to admit to, which are, as we say in the trade, not in plain sight?" the gnome asked.

"Pardon?"

"You can stare, lad, but you wouldn't believe the places some people embellish. We had one the other day, took three of us and an industrial torch to ..." The brunette coughed into her hand and the gnome almost smiled.

"Ah well, that's another story."

They then passed what looked like a weird hand-held vacuum cleaner over every inch of my body, before passing it over the contents of my pockets. My earrings and other assorted metal adornments were thrown in the bin.

I shrugged my shoulders and grinned.

"You look happy, lad, didn't you like them?"

"Not much," I admitted truthfully.

"Drunk were you?" asked the brunette, making a note on a pad of lined paper, which also displayed a multitude of little boxes, most of which she'd ticked.

I stared at the floor and shuffled my feet.

"I don't reckon he's ever been sober," Grumpy observed, turning a page on his clipboard.

"Right, the physical check was fine; now for the questions."

"No one ever expects the Spanish Inquisition," I uttered daftly.

"Bloody Monty Python," the gnome muttered, glaring at me. "And before you ask, the thumbscrews are in a box in the basement and they got polished last Thursday."

"Oh."

"Why are you here, business or pleasure?"

"I'm on holiday."

"You ever visited the Island before?"

"No."

"Have you been in contact with any animals over the past two weeks, apart from the duck?"

"No."

"Have you visited any farms or done any walking in the countryside over the last couple of days?"

"Do barges count?" I asked, a trifle hesitantly.

"Why?"

"Well I live on one, normally." I was given a look which clearly stated that neither of the inquisitors thought I was in any way normal.

"Did you leave the towpath?"

"Only to go to the shops, the launderette and the pub," I replied. "And we had to stop at one of the yards last week to have the toilet pumped out. Murdock said all it needed was a good kick but ..."

"That's all right as long as you didn't visit any farms," I was hurriedly advised.

The brunette moved towards me and to my horror I realized she was carrying a small hypodermic syringe.

"Argh!" I exclaimed, backing into the wall.

"It's all right lad, we just need a little blood to check you're not carrying any communicable disease, or have been indulging in any recreational drugs."

I began to sweat as the needle was inserted and nearly passed out as the hollow tube began to fill with rich red blood. A plaster and ball of cotton was gently applied to the hole left in my arm when the needle had finally been pulled from my quivering flesh. Meanwhile the gnome fed the carefully collected fluid into the machine.

After a couple of minutes the machine gave a high-pitched ping and a length of paper was carefully extracted from a slit in the side. This was read and then clipped to the rest of my notes.

"You can go now," the gnome advised. "Just one thing though, lad."

"What?"

"You'd better not drive for at least twenty-four hours, you're three times over the limit as it is."

"Um, no – I mean yes – er, thanks," I muttered as they opened a door in the blue-painted wall and ushered me into the rain-flecked air of Douglas Bay. All around me visitors and residents were emerging from a long row of painted metallic doors. Bob our driver was standing beside our coach, now neatly parked against the terminal building, and was checking passengers against his own list. I hurriedly boarded the brightly lit vehicle and collapsed into my seat with a surge of relief. After that Scotland would be a doddle.

Finally we arrived at our hotel, newly glittering and covered in more lights than Blackpool beach. Rooms were allocated and baggage delivered by a smartly dressed Chinese porter who spoke better English than I did. Clarris bounced on one of the single beds as the door closed, and laughed.

"We made it!"

"Did you notice that those four public school yobs from Slough didn't?" I muttered, walking to the window and our 'as advertised in the brochure page 23 sea view'.

"And it couldn't have happened to a nicer bunch," Clarris observed, remembering some of their less than savoury antics at the service station we'd stopped at before arriving at Heysham. The antics had involved pulling down their trousers and mooning at the passing traffic whilst one of them held a lighter and tried to light the less than savoury gasses they were excreting in noisy ‘parps’ of sound.

“Come on Edwin, if we push the beds together we can get at least six hours sleep before breakfast.”

“Six?” I asked, raising an eyebrow in disbelief.

“Well, five and a half then.”

chapter twenty-six

Of mice and men

The next morning we went down to breakfast shortly after Murdock and Mavis, although to be fair if it hadn't have been for Murdock banging on the door at seven thirty and shouting, "Are you two lazy sods up yet?" we would still have been cocooned in our soft, clean-smelling sheets and duvets until at least the early afternoon.

We arrived to find Murdock tucking into a plate piled high with bacon, sausage, eggs, mushrooms, fried bread and something circular and black.

"What is that?" I asked, pointing to the meaty disc.

"Black pudding," Murdock replied before taking a gulp of what looked like tea.

Mavis, who was silently dissecting a grapefruit, gave a short sarcastic laugh. "And if you think that's revolting you should have seen him eating the kipper he had as a starter."

Murdock gave her a fairly poisonous look and growled the word 'philistine', before resuming his mastication of the remaining fodder. At that point Pete arrived and settled into the seat next to Mavis; he too had a plate piled high with a variety of goodies and the smell wafting towards my nasal hairs had me immediately searching for the source of these essential supplies. At last I spotted the long white tablecloth-covered sideboard, which was positively groaning under a cornucopia of food. Clarris and I approached cautiously and spotting a lone pile of clean plates, grabbed one each and began to trawl through the breakfast menu. It was the sort of spread I'd only ever read about in books by P.G. Wodehouse. There was a huge pile of fruit, bowls of cereals, a silver platter of golden kippers and then a long metallic tray containing a huge variety of foods, all in separate compartments and all steaming gently. As we were trying to decide what to take first, a young man arrived with a fresh supply of fried eggs and long thin sausages. Clarris watched in growing fascination as I piled bacon, eggs, sausage, tomato and some rather good-looking kidneys on a plate.

"Aren't you having any?" I asked, trying to balance a plate of toast in my other hand.

"You really are going to eat all that, aren't you?" she stated.

"Yep."

"But what about your diet?"

"What diet?"

"Exactly." Clarris stood and glared at me, her arms folded; she looked for the first time exactly like my mother.

"Listen Clarris, for your information I have for the past few weeks eaten what I liked when I liked and I feel fitter than I have done for ages. If you want some health nut who enjoys rabbit food for breakfast and those sick-tasting yoghurt drinks, then go back to London."

I turned on my heel and stalked back to the table not

because I knew I'd scored a few points but because my food was getting cold and I hate cool egg white, especially with the fat coagulating at the edges. I would have laid money on Clarris returning with a bowl of fruit and a glass of orange juice, so it was with a certain amount of stunned amazement that I viewed her piled plate when she finally returned to our table. Clarris was going to eat every single banned item on our shopping list.

"Well, we don't get lunch do we?" Clarris remarked, ingesting a large piece of sausage.

I watched fascinated as she calmly carved into a round of black pudding.

"Do you know what that is made of?" Pete asked, his jaw lax with wonder.

"Yes. And I'd prefer you not to remind me as I happen to be a bit partial to it," Clarris replied, pouring herself a cup of tea from our shared teapot.

Mavis uttered a groan and pushed her bowl to one side.

"If you can't beat 'em join 'em," she growled, standing up and scooting off towards the buffet table.

She returned clutching a plate of scrambled eggs and sausage and we sat in companionable silence until the last triangle of toast had been filed away and the tea and coffee pots had been wrung dry.

"Right now, before Bob arrives to tell us which excursive delight he has planned for us today, it might be a very good idea for us to discuss our next move," Murdock announced, settling back into his chair.

Pete gave Clarris an odd look and cleared his throat. "I … er … had this friend who said he would take us by boat from the point of Ayre, which is the northernmost tip of the Island to Whithorn in Scotland for a small sum.

However he … er um …"

"We found out yesterday morning that he's also been in the custom of smuggling other things into Scotland apart from the odd human," Clarris added, avoiding direct eye contact with anyone.

"Drugs?" Murdock asked, looking more than a little disapproving.

"No. Cheap whisky." Pete paused. "From Taiwan," he added in an embarrassed whisper.

"You're joking!" Mavis squeaked.

"I never said he was very bright just that he had a boat, and frankly being a bit thick meant that he never asked who it was I wanted transported."

"Which is just as well if he's now helping Customs with their enquiries," Murdock stated bluntly.

"So what do we do now?" I asked.

"Have a good holiday?" Pete tentatively suggested.

We sat in silence broken only by Murdock who thoughtfully stroked his chin and then laughingly observed that at least now he could go on the steam train. Mavis grinned, getting into the swing of things, and added that she wouldn't mind the basking shark trip as the only basking sharks she'd ever seen were the ones working for the *Telegraph*.

It was at that point that Bob arrived resplendent in a blue and gold jacket with the sort of braided epaulets that had me wondering where he'd left his trumpet. He cleared his throat and when silence had been achieved announced that the excursion of the day was a trip to Laxey where we would enjoy the heady delights of the Snaefell mountain railway, the Laxey mines and the Lady Isabella.

When I asked who the Lady Isabella was and did she do teas, Murdock laughed in a derisive fashion and still chuckling, made his own escape. He was, he told Bob, off to see his dear old Mum as he'd spent many a formative year trooping round the Laxey mine workings on numerous school trips.

"I wonder if old rubber lips Quine is still in there," he mused, grinning evilly as he disappeared from view.

"Anybody else want to slack off?" Bob asked, bristling now that one of his flock had refused to be penned. There was another silence.

"Right, everyone on the bus and I'll point out the sights of interest as we go." Bob rubbed his hands, and then spotting the elderly couple and their Zimmer frame, amended his previous announcement.

"Of course, I don't mean right away, if you need to freshen up and grab your coats. Just remember I'm parked just outside the front entrance and I'll wait fifteen minutes before I blow a gasket and come and find you." This last quip wasn't aimed at the octogenarians but at a young pair of honeymooners who appeared to all intents and purposes to have been joined at the lips since we left Coventry.

I glanced briefly at Mavis, who was already rising from her chair, and then at Pete and Clarris. They all seemed to be quite pleased to be having a day off from our usual job of playing secret squirrel. Delighted at the recent turn in events and with a positive bounce in my trainers, I scurried off to my room for a quick spot of dental hygiene and to grab my warmest and most waterproof coat.

chapter twenty-seven

Flight

I stood below the huge Victorian waterwheel and waved at the three tiny figures clinging to the very top of the old spiral iron and brick staircase, a hundred or so feet above my head.

I had held my ground and declined to go up and see the astonishing view from the top, as eulogized at great length by the oracle of all things Manx, our driver Bob, who hadn't stopped talking since we'd left the confines of the hotel car park. Every fact, large, small and completely obscure was trotted out and even though we'd turned the overhead speakers off, some people hadn't managed to reach theirs and so the voice, though muted, carried on regardless.

Mavis and Clarris had laughed at my intransigence and Pete had gone so far as to do an impersonation of a chicken as he'd begun to climb. But I noticed after a while that no one else was joining them. Bob stood beside me, and pulling a packet of cigarettes from his pocket, took one out and lit it with an evil-smelling match.

"They'll be all right you know," he observed soothingly,

seeing the concern on my face as I looked up; it was giving me vertigo just looking at them. "As long as they don't look down."

"What do you mean?" I asked.

"What I said," was the muttered reply as Bob sloped off, looking ever so slightly guilty.

It took them a long time to come down, which gave me the opportunity to admire the huge wooden paddles of the great red and black painted wheel as it turned. Water dripped and gleamed as it made its relentless progress, the sound of the machinery a gentle dank lullaby.

Pete finally emerged, a pale and green-gilled shadow of his former self, supported on both sides by Mavis and Clarris.

"How was the view?" I asked innocently.

"Fine," they muttered in unison.

"Until he looked down," Mavis said as she gently eased him onto a waiting bench.

Clarris began to hunt around in the many pockets hidden in various parts of her voluminous coat and finally handed Pete a small silver hip flask, from which he gratefully took several large gulps, his hands trembling as he rescrewed the tiny cap back on afterwards.

"You all right?" I asked, laughter giving way to concern.

"It wobbled," he said finally with a shudder.

I looked up at the massive iron and brick construction proudly bearing the Manx symbol of three legs, united by a pair of dodgy knickers.

"It looks really solid," I stated.

"It wobbled," Pete reiterated with feeling.

"Oh good, you're back," Bob stated, arriving on the scene with a coterie of the more age-challenged of our group.

"We've just been down the old mine workings. It was very interesting, wasn't it?"

There was a group nod.

"Well, I'll just round up the others and then we can get back down to the village and the Snaefell mountain railway, although technically speaking it's an electric tram not a railway, built at the turn of the last century and still running. Very canny these Manx, never throw anything out if it still works, and why not is what I say? I'll be back in two shakes of a lamb's …" One of the old ladies coughed delicately and Bob astutely continued, "undercarriage. Sometimes I feel more like a bloody sheepdog than a driver," he announced to Mavis with a wink, as he set off back towards a distant grey slab of a building further up the hill.

"I think he fancies you," I observed, grinning at Mavis, who turned a dark beetroot and glared ferociously back.

"In his dreams," she spat.

"Quite possibly," I innocently agreed.

"There are times, Edwin dearest, when I could quite cheerfully …" Mavis stopped, realizing that two old biddies were waiting gleefully to hear what it was that she could do. A small child of about eight or nine who had been tossing stones into the small stream which ran beside the water wheel moved over to me and tugged on my sleeve.

"What?" I asked, looking down into the urchin's grimy face.

"She your sister?" he asked, giving me a view of bright white teeth and a variety of gaps.

"Er, yes."

"Thought so. I got one of them at home, she's a right pain too."

And with that sage announcement he picked up a large

piece of discarded slate and tossed it into the gurgling water, where it made a satisfying dull splash.

Mavis glared at him, and sensing that he might be in a fairly precarious position physically if not morally, he muttered "See yous" and scuttled off towards the road, hands deep in pockets and a tuneless whistle on his lips

"I hate kids," Mavis muttered.

"Oh I don't know, I quite like children really," Clarris observed. Mavis, Pete and I stood and stared at her, our mouths agape.

"I've just never managed to eat a whole one," Clarris laughed and began to wander back down to the coach park and our waiting vehicle.

"Pastry jacket and little dumpling buttons," Mavis agreed, catching her up.

Pete and I shared a fairly dumbfounded look as the enemies of the previous evening disappeared from view clutching onto each other's arms and giggling in that schoolgirl way that all women seemed to revert to when two or more were joined together.

Later, as we surveyed the entire island from a concrete platform set into the summit of the island's highest mountain and munched on freshly made sandwiches, and tentatively sipped from polystyrene cups of tomato soup, Mavis advised Pete and me that she and Clarris were going on a hunting trip and that we needn't wait up.

"Hunting trip?" I queried.

"Or talent scouting if you prefer," Clarris whispered in her sexiest voice.

Mavis giggled, sounding more like one of the St Trinians than a respected member of the press, although I use the term 'respected' loosely.

"Fine," Pete stated, "Edwin and I have something else planned."

"We do?" I mouthed at Pete.

Pete placed his finger against his nose and winked at me.

"Meet me in my room after dinner," he whispered as we stood in a line to board the returning tram.

I nodded my agreement and felt a frisson of satisfaction at Clarris's sudden desire to know what was going on, and for the rest of the afternoon spent a considerable amount of pleasurable time in not telling her anything at all. Which wasn't difficult, as I hadn't got a clue myself. What I did know, however, was that if Pete had remained true to his roots, it would involve some dark smoky room, jazz and a large volume of real beer.

As it happened I was almost right; the jazz turned out to be a local blues band, but the room was small and smoky and the beer was very real. I sat back and closed my eyes, almost feeling the soft and subtle riffs and quirky blasts of sound which ebbed and flowed from the small group of denim-clad musicians, as I began to finally enjoy my impromptu holiday.

Some four hours later Pete and I lurched back to the hotel. After much fumbling with keys and recalcitrant doorknobs we managed to gain our respective beds and to try to grab a few hours sleep. Clarris was already snoring on her side of the now joined beds and I was just falling off the rim of sleep when someone hammered loudly on the door, sending Clarris into a semi-comatose state of shock.

"Who the hell is that?" she asked, sitting bolt upright and clutching the lion's share of the duvet to her.

"How should I know?" I replied, turning my head into

my waiting pillow.

"Get up and find out," she hissed back at me, prodding my backside with a size seven foot.

Grudgingly and with a degree of reluctance which only the truly pissed can achieve, I padded over to the door and opened it. Murdock erupted into the room like an overactive volcano and began to open cupboards and drawers.

"What the ..." Clarris began with a certain amount of righteous indignation.

Murdock threw the backpack I'd left on the floor towards my feet with a well-aimed thump.

"For God's sake get up, get sober and get packed. You've got five minutes. I've got a car outside and a light aircraft waiting for the first rays of light at a disused airfield. And before you say anything else, Warwick and a few of his handpicked simians have already been spotted in a small but fast cruiser which is due to leave Liverpool at seven o'clock today bound for Douglas Bay. And my sources tell me he's armed and more than a little hacked off."

"Oh shit," Clarris groaned, now wide awake and fumbling with her underwear.

With a speed and agility I had no idea that I possessed, I was packed ready and waiting at the kerb outside our hotel four and a half minutes later.

Clarris was shivering beside me as Murdock emerged into the shadows of the partially lit car park and hastily beckoned us over to a waiting peoplecarrier. Mavis, Pete and Clarris clambered aboard as Murdock and I threw our meagre possessions in the back.

"Edwin, you can get in the front," Murdock ordered as he slunk into the driver's seat and turned on the ignition; within minutes we were on the mountain road and

Murdock, a look of grim determination chiselled into his features, was cornering at speeds which had been banned for years on the mainland. Nobody spoke at all during the drive, each person hanging grimly on to his or her seat and stomach, by the skin of their teeth.

Thirty minutes later we were scurrying across a black expanse of ancient tarmac to the ghostly moonlit silhouette of a small six-seater, single-engine plane. The pilot, a dour hunched figure who was prowling about under the wings with a small pencil torch, greeted us with a growl.

"About bloody time," he muttered. "And you can ditch the baggage, I only have enough fuel and lift for bodies with passports and cash."

Clarris made to demur but he silenced her with a look.

"Put it this way, you can take all that and we ditch the inflatable life-raft, which we may need as most of this journey will be made over the Irish Sea and the Western Isles or ..."

Slowly we each tossed our bags into the depths of a nearby drainage ditch, after first extracting every ounce of cash. Then we gingerly boarded the small plane, which swayed slightly as the wind began to pick up.

Silently we watched as our unnamed and never properly introduced pilot checked the numerous dials and controls which glowed faintly against the dashboard. As the first golden rays of light struck the ground, the engine roared into life, the propeller caught and held the cold air outside and we turned into the wind and took off. Wheels bouncing and juddering, finally the ground was left behind and we soared out over the northernmost tip of the Island. We flew very low and at barely a couple of hundred feet skimmed the Irish Sea. Ahead lay the indistinct shape of the place we hoped held the secret to my continued existence, Scotland.

chapter twenty-eight
Biggles

We skimmed across the dark, wave-flecked sea, our black elongated shadow cresting the cold water below us as we sped northwards, our pilot avidly pointing out things of interest over the internal radio, as we dipped and bucked in the freshening wind.

"Basking shark at nine o'clock," he announced after about five minutes. We looked out and saw the unmistakable dark hulk of something very large, moving between a small flotilla of sailing boats, their white sails straining against the air, green-edged foam frothing and boiling as they passed.

A little later we dipped our wings to a long, dark blue tanker plodding eastwards and saw ahead the corrugated green, brown and black outline of the approaching coast.

"I'm going to turn slightly over the Isle of Whithorn and then fly up through the low land around Port William and Ballantrae: it's fairly sparsely populated around there and as long as I avoid Stranraer and hug the coastline up to the Mull of Kintyre and then around the smaller islands until we get to Mull, we should be able to sneak into North Connell airfield."

"And where exactly is North Connell?" Mavis asked as we sped ever northwards, sunlight glinting brightly on the jagged black rocks not very far below.

"Just outside Oban," our pilot replied, suddenly banking steeply as he changed his heading to avoid what looked like a mountain looming at us out of the early morning mist.

"Oban," Pete repeated, fishing a folded map from his pocket.

"That is what I said, young man. Now if you've no further questions I'd like to concentrate on my flying, that is if you want to avoid both the Scots version of radar and ditching in the sea. Of course we could hit a bit of rock – do any of you have any preference over a dry or wet landing?"

After that we kept silent and hung onto the armrests and each other as the little plane weaved and wobbled around the convoluted coastline. It was surprising really how much of the land was actually higher than we were. In fact it was rather like one of those video games where the space pilot has to outmanoeuvre thousands of aliens while avoiding being blasted out of the sky by something resembling a giant squid with attitude and a jet pack. Unfortunately it differed in that you couldn't press the pause button while you made a cup of tea and grabbed a chocolate digestive.

It was with a certain amount of relief that we finally spotted a large field with what looked like a windsock at the end. Our pilot circled gently, and then, after lining up the long strip of green with what looked like a caravan site but turned out to be a collection of decomposing huts and small hangars, landed with a bump and a squeal of flaps.

Shakily we crawled from the plane and stood shivering, still half-asleep and more than a little hung-over, under a large awning attached to a long low trailer. Weeds were sprouting from the roof and a dark reddish brown stain had dribbled down one side of a solitary picture windowframe. Without warning a door in the wall opened and a nervous looking man in a dark green anorak emerged blinking into the morning sunshine.

"Good morning, Douglas," our pilot remarked as he climbed out of the plane.

"Morning, Sir Timothy," the man replied, plodding towards him, a large brown paper wrapped parcel clutched to his chest.

"You got the malt I ordered?" Sir Timothy asked, licking a finger and holding it out in the seaweed-scented breeze.

"Aye and here's the side of best salmon for the missus."

"Good man. Is Towser around? I need to refuel and get back before She Who Must Not Be Blamed needs this blasted fish. Why in God's name she has to go and arrange dinner for twenty at a moment's notice, I have no bloody idea. I mean, it's only a birthday for God's sake, and it's not as if it's a one-off. Besides, I was hoping to get in a round of golf before taking the dogs for a run." Our pilot snorted with indignation and blew into his moustache.

"He'll be here in about ten minutes, you can wait inside if you like. I've got a bit of best back sizzling nicely on the primus."

Sir Timothy rubbed his hands gleefully together and then turned and glared at us.

"Well, don't you have people to avoid?" he barked, eyebrows bristling.

"Er, yes," Murdock replied, before shooing us towards a gate at the end of the field.

"Thanks a lot Biggles, I owe you one," Murdock shouted as we ambled off.

Sir Timothy waved at our departing backs before disappearing, the fleeting aroma of smokey bacon cut off as the metal door clanged shut behind him.

Above us curlews called and a rabbit scampered across the short nibbled grass which ran in an uneven line from the gate to a glimpse of dark road. Murdock began to speed up as the sound of a diesel van with exhaust problems reached our ears.

"Come on," he urged. "We really don't want to be seen."

Suddenly galvanised, we sprinted through the wire mesh gate and dived into the neighbouring shrubbery just as the van roared into view. Panting, we crouched down, our bodies touching and waited for Murdock to give us the all clear. But instead Murdock began to half crawl, half stagger through a sea of ruffled bracken and lethally sharp briar bushes. We reluctantly followed, and finally emerged at the edge of a deserted main road, scratched, bitten and extremely hungry. My stomach rumbled loudly in the sun-drenched silence.

"You hungry, lad?" Murdock enquired.

"Starving," I replied.

"Well, you'll be pleased to know that at the end of this road is a delightful garage-cum-general store which also does a bloody good all day breakfast."

"You don't mean one of those huge, cholesterol-covered, protein rich, heart attack inducing plates of animal products you insist on starting the day with?" Clarris asked.

"Yes."

"Good, I could eat a horse," Clarris declared, smacking

her lips with undisguised pleasure at the thought of the approaching feast.

Murdock grinned at her and began to trot off along the ditch-edged path running beside the road. We followed in a straggle, not talking, our minds bent on our respective bodily needs.

Three miles down the road we were offered a lift from a passing minibus half full of students, the roof covered in a motley assortment of slim, sharply pointed canoes and the back with a rack of variously rusting bikes.

After joining them in a few choruses of rudely but very imaginatively amended variations of a Will Young classic helped along with several cans of lager and a strangely smelling, fat, hand-rolled cigarette, we were deposited at the McTavish service station.

An aroma of astonishing goodness met our nostrils, and drooling like a bunch of bloodhounds after an escaped convict, we scuttled into the neon-signed café for the full Scottish. Murdock ordered the food in a surprisingly good imitation of a Scottish bricklayer and flirted outrageously with the amply endowed waitress. The rest of us kept quiet until she had moved off and then we went into the sort of huddle that gave rugby a bad name until it was banned altogether.

"So what do we do now?" Clarris hissed.

"We have something to eat and then we walk back towards Oban," Murdock stated, digging holes in the sugar with a toothpick.

"Why? What's so special about Oban?" Mavis asked.

"Well, firstly, it's the gateway to the isles and so there are a lot of people all milling around waiting to get on or off the various ferries which means that we won't look out of place, like we do here." Murdock dug a brown crystalline blob out of the sugar bowl and carefully placed it on the tablecloth.

"I mean to say," he continued, "around here they might get one or two strange faces but not five at the same time."

"And the other reason?" Mavis prompted.

"It has a mainline railway station, where we should be able to get a ticket all the way up to Inverness."

"And what if we can't?" Pete enquired, carefully folding his napkin into a series of geometric shapes.

"Well let's just pray that we can, because it's a bloody long way to walk."

Our food arrived at that point, the only visible difference from the full Manx being that a slice of black pudding had been replaced by a slice of fried haggis, or at least I hoped that was what it was.

We ate in a companionable and stolid silence and after the last morsel had been chewed and swallowed, sat clutching our warm mugs of creosote-coloured tea.

"How far is it to Oban?" I asked, rubbing my ankle with the toe of my other foot. The blisters I thought I'd managed to rid myself of seemed to be trying to make a return and it hurt.

"Not far," Murdock stated airily, avoiding eye contact.

"As the crow flies," Mavis muttered. Murdock gave her the look and retreated into grumpiness.

"Well, little Miss Perfect, have you got any better ideas?" he growled.

"No."

"I don't see why we are going to Inverness though." Clarris mused. "I thought the chap we are after was in Edinburgh?"

"He was but according to a mate fairly high up in MISS ..."

"Who?"

"The Manx Internal Security Services. Someone has had him moved to a place called Fort George, which frankly is going to be a complete pig of a place to get into."

"How would they have known that?" Pete queried.

"Because they keep a very close and concerned eye on his movements. You see, Pete, if he gets into a position of real power he could reclaim the Island as Crown property and nobody wants that; they certainly don't want to risk losing their lucrative position in the financial or tourism stakes and as a major part of their income is within the import-export field they certainly don't want Whitehall sniffing around for their cut."

"Import-export?" Clarris sniffed. "You mean smuggling, don't you?"

"So what if I do? The Isle of Man has been doing it off and on for centuries, in fact we got kind of expert in it," Murdock observed, thoughtfully scratching at the stubble under his chin.

"And how do we pay to get there? To say nothing of replenishing our non-existent wardrobes?" Mavis asked, hastily changing the subject. Murdock gave her a grateful look and suddenly produced a wad of bills.

"Where the hell did you get that kind of cash?" Pete asked with a short whistle as he also realized, as I did, that they were the real thing – they were in fact Scottish notes.

"This is a sort of loan."

"From whom?" Clarris whispered as Murdock began to hastily hand round wads of cash.

"Er ... the Isle of Man Government."

"Why?" Mavis asked, nervously swallowing as we each

began to realize just how big this so-called loan was. We each had a hundred pounds and Murdock had hardly made a dent in his roll of paper, some of which appeared to be in denominations of fifty. Murdock looked even more shifty and ignored her questioning and anxious look.

"That money is for a set of clothes and essential items. We can get the other stuff like walking boots and proper equipment when we get to Inverness, as frankly we will look less suspect if we just appear to be on a daytrip ... or maybe visiting friends at the university would be our best storyline." Murdock paused and then added in a harsher tone, "Look Clarris. Nobody really wants to change the current status quo you know, despite what this bastard Warwick and his little mates are saying."

"Really?" Clarris snorted, looking totally unconvinced.

"Really. Oh come on, think about it; the thing isn't perfect but it works. Crime is down, drugs kept to a bare known minimum, educational standards are higher than they've ever been, you can actually fall down the stairs and get a bed and a surgeon the same day and the trains run on time. I might not like the so-called nanny state but it's a damm sight better than the last one."

We sat and drained the last of the tea and then ambled off to the toilets, our minds thinking their own but surprisingly similar thoughts, while Murdock settled the bill.

Outside we sat in a row by the kerb and kicked the gravel thrown up by the sparse traffic. After about ten minutes Murdock finally emerged clutching a selection of brown paper bags.

"Lunch," he declared, handing us one each before ambling off down the road without even bothering to see if we were following.

chapter twenty-nine

The Flying Scotsman

We arrived in Oban, hot, tired and smelling strongly of animal byproducts. A friendly soul driving a tractor with a straw-covered trailer had offered us a lift. It might have had something to do with the milk of human kindness but I had a sneaky feeling, confirmed in part by Murdock's whisper of "dirty-minded bastard", that it had more to do with the sparsity and size of the clothes that both Clarris and Mavis had peeled down to in the heat of the day.

The girls were invited, with a big lecherous smile, to climb up into the front, while we lesser mortals were given the grunted nod and fluttered hand signal, to clamber onto the trailer. It was only as the tractor picked up speed and rattled off, that we realized it wasn't just straw.

"Do they have any washing facilities at the station?" I asked, holding a handkerchief to my nose.

"Don't know, but it's warm and there's always the sea."

"Oh."

I realized that Murdock was in one of his less than helpful moods and that Pete was having a bit of a think. During our time together in the flat, this had on occasion taken days. So, reaching the conclusion that no one really wanted to indulge in a bit of idle banter, I sat on the edge of the trailer with my legs dangling over the sides and began to drink in my first real views of this strange northern country.

Most of it seemed to go up and the bits that didn't were surrounded by water. Houses and small squat white cottages hugged the roadside. Washing billowed from clothes lines and strange-looking hairy cattle grazed the lush green grass edging the water, which I was reliably informed was a sea loch.

"Loch Etive," Murdock informed me, coming up for air and pointing towards the vast expanse of aquamarine fluid. "Contains the best bloody mussels I've ever had."

Murdock smacked his lips expressively and with a pensive shake of the head settled back into his own thoughts. I had come to the conclusion that Murdock's travelling around the globe had memories containing one of two things, either the quality of the beer or the food.

I was almost asleep when Pete gave me a hefty nudge with the point of his elbow. Startled, I blearily blinked into the sudden glare of the midday sun and realized our tractor was surrounded on all sides by elderly guesthouses and neatly trimmed hedges. Signs hung at every angle extolling the virtues of each house of rest, varying from welcomes to animals and children to one promising hot water in every room.

As we progressed down the hill, closely followed by a convoy of steadily simmering drivers, I got my first glimpse of Oban and the islands beyond. Boats of every size and shape were milling around, either leaving or entering the bay. Horns blared and whistles rang as they crossed and re-crossed the invisible sea lanes. Land rose in a green and grey ridge opposite and beyond soared higher peaks of purple and indigo blues.

Finally the tractor pulled into a parking bay opposite the black-railed promenade and after being given a grateful kiss by both Clarris and Mavis our red-faced driver helped us down onto the pavement. Murdock muttered something and passed him a couple of notes, which were received with a wink and a silently tapped nose.

We watched as he chugged off down the road and vanished behind a large lorry from Aberdeen. Murdock and Pete stood together and then after a few minutes of close-faced huddle began to walk off towards the docks and a large blue and green ferry. We followed, straggling across the pavement and every so often stopping to let either a motorized wheelchair or small child whizz past. One old man almost knocked me down as he soared towards us and then onwards, followed by an elderly lady who I took to be his wife and a large man in a white suit and running shoes.

Shops and restaurants spread out on either side and Murdock, spotting a large department store opposite, stopped abruptly and beckoned us towards him. When we were neatly assembled, he addressed us in the authoritarian tones and clearly enunciated vowels of a teacher about to release the remnants of a school trip onto an unsuspecting world.

"Right, you've got an hour and a half to get some new clobber; you see that big glass building next to the Ferry terminal and that big brown and green floating shoe box, aptly entitled 'The Bonny Prince'?" We all nodded.

"That's the station. I'll be waiting near the ticket office

and if you manage to get there any earlier there's a small café next to the platform and I'll get you a sandwich. I don't know about you lot but I really don't fancy this very much." So saying, he tossed the brown paper bag, now a definitely darker brown in colour, into the nearest litterbin. Pete and I followed suit.

We looked pointedly at Clarris, who shrugged and explained that she and Mavis had already shared their lunch with the driver of the tractor, who it turned out was called Hamish and under all those clothes had a physique of the average professional football player. They were still giggling and making totally uncalled for, in my opinion salacious comments about Hamish and his well-earned nickname. Which, incidentally, they refused to divulge before they both scooted off towards a ladies' dress shop on the other side of the road.

Pete wandered away to my left and Murdock to my right. It felt rather odd to be suddenly bereft of company after being surrounded by people twenty-four hours a day. I let the novel feeling of loneliness and peace settle around me; it was truly wonderful. So much so, that I almost skipped across the busy street and into the nearest store selling a variety of clothing for tourists and kilt fanciers.

An hour later I wandered into the railway station, after visiting the gentlemen's toilets on the quayside, dressed in a pair of new jeans, sweatshirt, trainers and grime-free underwear. I'd also acquired a pair of reflective wrap-around sunglasses, which made me look like some turn-of-the-century American law enforcer. Murdock instantly spotted me and beckoned me to a plastic umbrella-shaded table.

"Where in God's name did you get those things?" he asked, jabbing at my ornamental eyewear with a crumb-flecked digit.

"Oxfam. They were in the window and I couldn't resist," I replied, eyeing the last wedge of sandwich nestling in the remains of what looked like a plate of mixed salad.

"Stop drooling, lad, and grab yourself something from the cold cabinet over there – here this should cover it." Murdock handed me a handful of heavy coins and went back to the pleasurable task of draining his pint-sized glass of brown froth.

I was halfway through a prawn and egg baguette when Pete turned up, resplendent in a lime green shirt complete with red and yellow palm trees, and a white straw hat. Murdock and I gave a synchronized cough of mutual horror and Pete grinned.

"What do you think? Is this touristy enough for you?"

"Sod off and get something to eat," Murdock admonished, screwing his eyes up in a parody of pain before pressing a screwed-up note into Pete's hand.

"I've got one extra from 'Men in Black' and the bleeding tailor of Panama so far – any bets on what bubble and squeak will turn up as?" he asked, scooping up the last of the cress.

Almost immediately his question was answered by two visions of loveliness; both were wearing matching sleeveless tops with a jumper knotted around the shoulders. But it was the short pleated skirts that the male eye naturally turned to.

"Bloody hell, Clarris, you've not got bad legs for a ..."

There was a short pause as we also took in the matching high-heeled sandals and ankle socks.

"What's with the socks?" I asked.

"Fashion statement," Mavis replied, before spotting our now empty plates.

"Victim more like," muttered Murdock, handing them some cash and with the words "you've got fifteen minutes" pointed them in the direction of the sandwich counter.

Exactly fourteen minutes later we ambled off towards Platform 2 and our waiting train. Smoke bellied out from between the metal wheels and soot-scented steam hissed from the smoke stack above the engine. Pete watched in disbelief and then hurried off towards the gleaming engine to take a better look. He found us in a carriage halfway down the train, just before a grey and gold-uniformed guard blew his whistle and waved the green flag he was carrying.

"Do you know what this is?" he chuckled excitedly as he settled himself next to the window and glued his face against the glass.

"Nope," I replied, taking another look at the cards I held cradled in my hands. I had two kings and an ace already and this was only the first hand.

"*The Flying Scotsman*!" he shrieked.

I looked up at him with a puzzled expression.

"So?"

"You know?"

"Know what?" I asked, picking up another ace and a three; things were definitely looking up.

"Never mind," Pete muttered dreamily as the train gave a lurch and with a sudden loud grating noise of metal on metal, slid out from under the platform canopy and into the waiting gloom of our first tunnel.

chapter thirty

A slight detour

The train hissed, rumbled and whistled its way across bridges, under trees and past vapour-wreathed castles. We stopped with a groan at every station to offload boxes and people and to take on even more boxes and interesting crates, some of which either squealed or clucked in bad temper.

It was at one of these stops just when the card game was beginning to hot up, that Murdock leant out of the window and then with a suitable expletive grabbed the cards and hastily opened the carriage door. We followed in complete disarray and just about managed to fall onto the waiting platform before the great train gave a gargantuan snort and chuffed and huffed into the distance.

"What was all that about?" Clarris asked, adjusting the strap of her sandal, much to the appreciation of a large man with a beard who was loading bags of cabbages onto a small handcart.

"This is Crianlarich," Murdock informed us, pointing at the sign above our heads.

"So?" Mavis snapped.

Mavis had been just about to win the biggest pot of the journey and was understandably more than a little cheesed off about having to call it a day.

"We have to change here to get to Fort William."

"And …" Mavis prompted, her face set with the same sort of stony look that got Medusa and her snakes such a bad press.

"Then we take the New Mountain Railway down through the Great Glen and right into the heart of Inverness."

"The New Mountain Railway?" Pete repeated in tones of awe.

"Aye, otherwise we would have had to have gone to Glasgow, changed, got on a train to Edinburgh, changed, got on another to Perth, changed, and then we might have managed to make the connection with the main train to Inverness. Which would, all things being equal, have taken about four days, possibly longer, by which time our particular quarry would in all likelihood have been spirited away to some other even more inaccessible location."

"And this way is better?" Clarris asked, looking around the now deserted platform.

"Yes," Murdock replied, a glint of defiance in his eyes. I hoped for his sake that a train came along within the next hour, or from the expression on Clarris and Mavis's faces he would be wearing his teeth on the outside.

"You waiting for something?" a voice asked. We turned to the speaker and realized the man with the beard had returned. This time he had a cart piled high with what looked and smelt like smoked fish.

"The train to Fort William," Murdock replied, "the one due in at four thirty."

"But this is Tuesday," the man stated.

"So?"

"Well the four thirty runs on Mondays and Thursdays."

"And this is Tuesday," I said, speaking the words out loud. They didn't sound any better but at least the knife-edged silence had been broken.

"But there must be another train," Murdock squeaked. For a big man he could reach all the way up to soprano when he tried.

"Well, there's the freight in ten minutes," the man said, thoughtfully scratching his thigh.

"We'll catch that then," Murdock announced.

"But you can't; it's a freight train, there ain't no room for passengers."

"I'll pay," Murdock stated, firmly pressing a wad of notes into the bearded one's hands. "Cash."

"Aye well, it's you who will be uncomfortable, not me. Just don't let that idiot Rebus stick this little lot anywhere warm." He pointed at the cart of fish just as we could hear the distant diesel purr of an approaching engine.

When the *Beast of the Borders* had finally arrived and stopped (the first time it overshot the platform and had to be reversed slowly, the engine belching plumes of evil-smelling smoke as it inched its way into the correct position), we stood and stared for a good thirty seconds before Murdock came to and we were introduced to the 'idiot Rebus', a callow youth of about eighteen with spiky red hair and a gormless expression, the expression changing to one of rampant lust the moment he caught a glimpse of Clarris's knickers, as she bent to adjust the strap of her sandal again.

After that Clarris was given the best and only seat next to a small heater, which she was invited to share with Mavis whose skirt he had gleefully discovered was just as short. The rest of us had to perch on a varying selection of crates, with the possible exception of the one containing the fish and the big reinforced one which growled whenever you got any nearer than a couple of feet. The rest of the journey up through the Highlands was spent in the semi-darkness, playing cards and trying to keep warm.

Many hours later the train came to a complete stop and Rebus opened the door of the van and peered out.

"What's going on?" Pete asked.

"Dunno," Rebus replied, "we don't normally stop here."

Rebus, prodded in the back by Murdock, grudgingly mooched up to the engine where a group of people were standing around talking in a soft but animated fashion. Rebus said something to them and then ran back towards us and breathing hard, leapt back into the van.

"There are police at the next stop, searching all the trains," Rebus squawked.

"Why?" Pete asked.

"Dunno."

"So who stopped the train?" Clarris prompted, as Rebus began to unearth a pile of smaller cardboard boxes from the far corner. Most of them rattled and those that didn't clinked.

"McDonald and Sinclair from Inverlair." As if on cue, two worried-looking faces, covered in a variety of facial hair, appeared at the opening of the guard's van.

"You found them yet, Rebus lad?" one asked.

"Yes," Rebus answered, thrusting a box at them.

"If you give us a lift we'll help you unload," Pete offered.

"Aye, we could do with some help. Can't take you further than the village though," the thinner of the two replied, grabbing a box and moving off into the twilit gloom. It was surprising just how many boxes found their way onto the Ford Transit parked as near to the tracks as possible – all of them travelling at what I guessed was far less than the going rate normally required by the administrators in Edinburgh. This fact was confirmed by the handing over of a plain brown envelope on completion of the box transfer. Steam and mist mingled as the handing over ceremony was carried out under the eagle eyebrows of the senior engine driver and a large guy with an even larger shovel held at a threatening angle until the envelope's content were checked and most of the notes had been held over the bright white light of a high wattage, industrial strength torch.

Cash on delivery having been confirmed with a small discount being agreed due to having to stop short of the actual station, we all piled into the back of the van and stood propped up by a variety of packages and assorted crates until the short drive was over. When the engine was finally killed and the doors opened we found ourselves in a well-lit courtyard.

"Come on, throw us the stuff," a querulous voice shouted from the depths of a large hole in the ground.

"In for a penny, in for a pound," Murdock muttered, picking up a crate from the floor of the van and hefting it towards the hands poking from the rim of the abyss.

"Ta," the voice grunted.

Half an hour later we sat in the warm and steamy confines of a saloon bar and tucked hungrily into plates of mashed potato, swede and a peppery heap of meat and oatmeal.

"Ah, the haggis," Murdock drooled, his fork poised over the pungent remains. He then began to quote something in some sort of mangled and totally unintelligible accent before plunging his knife into the black and grainy mound. There was a smattering of appreciative applause from McDonald and Sinclair who were rearranging the bar and alternately serving the few customers propping up the counter. The only other body present was a large black dog, lying in a position of complete abandonment in front of the fire, which smoked and warmed in equal measure.

When we'd finished, Murdock extracted a long fat cigar from the pockets of his newly acquired jacket and with the ease of experience, cut, lit and finally puffed it into smelly red-tipped life. Clarris coughed and glared at him, expecting a mass chorus of disapproval to back her up. Nothing happened, except that Pete lit a foul-smelling long black cigarette and Sinclair came and sat down next to us, bearing an ornately carved, deep-bowled pipe and a brown hessian drawstring bag. We watched in silence as he scooped large flakes of gold-flecked tobacco into the bowl of the pipe and then bending low, lit and fanned it into smoky life.

"Aye, there's nothing better than a good honest pipe at the end of a hard day," Sinclair announced with a hefty sigh.

"That there isn't," Murdock agreed, sitting back and sending a ring of smoke up towards the tar-coloured beamed ceiling.

"So where are you from?" McDonald asked, arriving beside our table bearing a large bottle of whisky and a motley collection of small square-edged glasses.

"The Isle of Man," Murdock replied.

"You Manx?" Sinclair asked, black beetle eyes glinting.

"Half and half. Mother was Scots, a Donaldson from

Dumfries, father was Manx."

"Good mix." Sinclair nodded his shaggy head approvingly before adding in less friendly tones, "Your companions on the other hand need a bit more explaining."

Murdock shuffled and we all drew further into the wall. McDonald, who had flexed his shoulder muscles in a good imitation of an irate walrus with toothache, now picked up a long polished two-edged sword from its resting place on the rough plastered wall. It had a funny bit on the end and looked at first glance like a flattened axe. With great deliberation and the dawn of a grin, he gently and with deliberate slowness rubbed the gleaming blade with the hem of his shirt cuff.

Pete and I both gulped at the same time; we'd heard a lot of stories about the Scots and their longstanding dislike of the English. Now was not the time to see if the myth was true.

"Perhaps I ought to explain," Murdock stated, totally at ease.

"Aye, that might be an idea," Sinclair agreed, pulling the bottle towards him and extracting the cork with his teeth.

"This young chap here is young Edwin Snipe, wanted by at least four police forces for the anarchistic and free use of fire-starting liquids."

Sinclair grinned at me. "Aye, I thought I recognized the face. Any enemy of that bloody girly government is a friend indeed – drink up lad." A very full glass was placed in front of me. I took a careful sip and fire raced down my throat.

"Very nice," I croaked.

"This is Pete, one of my old Special Forces buddies and a good man in a scrap." Pete was passed another full glass and downed it in one without so much as a startled whimper.

There was an appreciative pause before more was poured. “Take the next one at a more gentle pace, man, it needs to be supped slowly,” McDonald admonished, still nursing his instrument of persuasion.

“This young lady is Mavis Wordsworth, the scourge of Whitehall and half-sister to young Edwin here.”

“A writer, eh? I’ve read some of your stuff – you don’t like anyone much do you lass?”

“No.”

“Aye well, you’re still young. You’ll learn soon enough where a woman’s real place is.” Sinclair gave her a blatantly lustful look before pushing a smaller pouring of malt to her. McDonald, however, leant over and stopped her from picking it up with a large hairy hand.

“Just a minute, Angus, she may be a wee woman but she has the waspish tongue of my great Aunt Moira, another writer feared by governments everywhere, so the lass deserves an equal portion. Besides she’s a journalist and can probably drink you under the table.”

More fluid was poured into the small glass until it threatened to overflow. Mavis took a small sip and then with a lick of pink-tinged lips, a hefty slug.

Clarris wriggled in her seat and looked towards the door.

“And so who’s the other lassie then?” Sinclair asked.

“Aye well, I’m glad you asked me that because I don’t altogether approve but there’s no accounting for taste.” Murdock paused and took another nip.

I wondered how long it would take to bury our bodies when Murdock continued.

“She’s Edwin’s bint. Silly tart insists on going with us but ...” His voice tailed off, giving the listener the impression that I was not only henpecked but one sandwich short of a picnic. Clarris gave him a look of pure vitriol laced with a small amount of admiration; after all it takes one expert liar to admire the handiwork of another, and grabbed her drink.

"Well that seems to cover the formalities of introduction but unless you can give us a pretty good reason as to why you are the wrong side of the wall none of you will be leaving tonight or any other, at least not with your full quota of appendages," McDonald promised, sitting back in his chair and pointing a small snub-nosed revolver at us. I had no idea where the weapon had come from but as the remaining two members of the bar were also pointing a variety of guns at us, I had no reason to disbelieve him.

"Perhaps you all ought to sit down, after all this could take a long time," Murdock announced in his most reasonable tones, and then calmly leaving the bits involving Clarris and Pete out, told the truth, the whole truth and mostly nothing but the truth to a steadily silent and totally gobsmacked audience.

Two and a half bottles later he'd finished. Mavis lay asleep over the table and Pete and I were having a lot of difficulty in keeping upright. Clarris had departed behind the bar to work the coffee machine and Sinclair looked like a haddock with lockjaw.

It was some time later when the coffee was beginning to take the edge off the whisky-induced mental fug that McDonald finally spoke.

"So how can we help?" he asked, grinning from ear to bristle-covered ear.

chapter thirty-one

Of myths and legends

"You want to help?" Clarris squeaked in total disbelief.

"Aye."

"Why?" Clarris asked.

"Why not? You ask a lot of questions for a tart." Sinclair muttered, giving her a thoughtful look.

"Well I just thought that you'd be a bit more on the side of ..."

"Some bastard who wants to be king just because his parents met on a very dark night, performed the sexual act in a haze of herbal baccy and never met again? To say nothing of that prick Warwick."

"You've heard of him?" Pete asked.

"Aye, 'the puppet meister' – even the *Scotsman* has had a few wee digs at the man and not because the slimy git is English either," McDonald informed us, pouring himself a second cup of coffee.

"It's because he's a slimy git," Sinclair stated to a nod of heads from the corner settle near the fire, now merely a few forlorn embers and a lot of grey ash.

" I mean to say, we've not done too badly without a king for the last three or four hundred years and in my view if it ain't broke why fix it?" he added a trifle unsteadily.

"Besides, we've almost got that lot down in Edinburgh housetrained and that's taken nigh on thirty years – seems a bit daft starting it all over again for some mad prat and his idea of Svengali," McDonald remarked, before getting up and replacing the long metal weapon upon the wall.

"What is it?" I asked, airily pointing in the general direction of the heavy armament, as its handle was inserted back in its leather strap.

"That, lad, is what is called a Claymore. Or it's Hollywood's idea of one. My dad got a part as an extra in the Mel Gibson fiasco and took this as part of his pay. Looks good though and the tourists love that sort of thing."

"Tourists?" Mavis asked, vaguely puzzled. "I thought the borders were closed?"

"Aye they are to you English but we're always ready to entertain the Europeans or the yanks or them antipodeans. Spend a lot they do and you wouldn't believe some of the verbal diarrhoea that old Lexus McTavish can produce on a good day with the wind behind him." There was a chuckle from the settle in the corner, and even the dog opened one eye and yawned in agreement.

"So Scotland has never really closed?" Clarris asked in amazement.

"No. Why should it? We need the cash same as the next person, nothing to stop anyone coming or going. Just as long as they understand that this is our country and we won't be bossed around by some soft southern bitch with an axe to grind," Sinclair hissed, looking Clarris straight in the eyes.

Clarris glared back at him and then with a swift glance at me lowered both glittering orbs and muttered, "And why should you?"

"Why indeed?" McDonald echoed, thoughtfully looking from me to Clarris and back again; whatever it was that he thought he saw seemed to satisfy him because he began to gather up cups and glasses almost happily.

"Well if you really want to help," Murdock began in a soft undertone, "you could get us onto the next train to Inverness."

"Inverness?" Sinclair glanced at McDonald, who seeing the puzzled looks on our faces, suddenly snorted with laughter.

"There is no train to Inverness."

"But the new …" Pete began.

"Mountain Railway?" Sinclair laughed outright as he finished off Pete's sentence.

"You shouldn't believe all you read, laddie. I'd have thought that was second nature travelling around with a bunch of bloody reporters."

"So what happened? It was in all the papers, how it was started using the latest technology, it was to be one of the fastest and most reliable overhead electric tram systems ever built."

"Aye well, you lot down in London had the Olympics and we had the bloody railway."

Sinclair placed some freshly cleaned cups and mugs on the table together with a variety of biscuits still in their cardboard and plastic wrappings. "Oh they started building it all right, until they realized they were either going to have to blow the sides off half the bloody mountains around Loch Ness, or use the existing road and build a new one costing twice as much. In the end they decided to appoint some committee to look into the possibilities – that was five or maybe ten years ago and we have nae heard a dickey bird since."

"And that's it?" Pete asked, scandalized.

"Aye."

"My cousin up at Strone reckons our Nessie made 'em an offer they couldn't refuse and their bones lie bleaching at the bottom of the loch," the sage on the settle informed us.

"Your idiot of a cousin would," Sinclair snorted, pouring out yet more coffee, which slunk from the pot to the cup as if still alive.

"There, drink that, it'll put fur on your tongues," he added, settling himself back in his chair and unwrapping a sugar-dusted fat finger of shortbread.

"No, what you need is a lift down to Inverness by boat."

"Old Charlie!" McDonald exclaimed suddenly. "That's who you need."

"Who the hell is old Charlie?" Murdock asked, helping himself to a chocolate bourbon.

"My nephew's father-in-law. He runs the *Nessie Rose* – it's a small motor cruiser which the tourist board have on a sort of charter."

On the words 'sort of charter' there was the sound of a universal titter.

"What sort of charter?" Mavis asked.

"Never you mind, lassie," Sinclair admonished. "I'll get on the radio and get him to pick you up at the old landing stage up the road a mile or two. I'm sure he'll take the lot of you for a spot of cash."

McDonald whispered something to Sinclair, who then

leant over to Murdock. After about five minutes of quiet negotiation terms were agreed and Murdock ambled off with McDonald to find the radio, which by the way they disappeared from view behind the bar, appeared to be located in the cellar.

After another short wait during which I managed to find my way to the toilets and back without staggering too much or falling over, they finally returned. Sinclair, at a nod from McDonald, disappeared, returning with a rucksack each and warm coats for Clarris and Mavis. He also bore five sets of oddly coloured waterproofs and several flasks.

"For the journey," he announced as he handed over the items in exchange for a large wad of rolled-up notes.

Some ten minutes later we sat in small tired heaps in the back of the old Ford as Sinclair drove us off to our next rendezvous point. Yawning continuously, I was pushed and pulled onto a badly lit slippery deck and manhandled down a sagging wooden ladder and into a canvas hammock smelling oddly of fresh lavender and old socks. I was too tired to protest and too drunk to think, so with the room swaying slightly I closed swollen eyes and snored my way into oblivion.

Hours later I was rudely woken by someone throwing something wet over my nose. Startled, I sat bolt upright and nearly knocked myself out on the ceiling, which was a mere six inches from my gently rocking bed.

"Edwin, you all right?" asked a deep voice. It was Murdock.

"I suppose so," I replied groggily, rubbing the growing bump on my forehead. "What time is it?"

"Nearly five o'clock. We should be passing Urquhart Castle by the time it starts to get dark. We've already gone through the Caledonian Canal."

"You and your bloody canals," I groaned.

"Now then lad, now then, let's have no fighting. It's been a lovely day. Pete and I even caught a couple of fish."

"Good for you."

"What you need is a lot of fresh air, a nice cup of tea, something to eat and something useful to do." Murdock patted me on the back and then half tipped, half pulled me from the snug confines of my hammock.

I clambered up the rickety ladder and emerged into a freshening wind which whipped my hair and made me shiver. Mavis, wrapped in her new waterproofs, gave me a grin and a mug of brown liquid. Pete handed me a sandwich and Murdock dumped a huge mass of black glistening rubber at my feet. It looked like about thirty foot of inner tube.

"What's this?" I asked, kicking it.

"Never you mind," Murdock said, handing me what looked like an antique foot pump.

"All you have to do is blow it up."

"Blow it up?" I repeated.

"All of it." Murdock replied. "Mavis says you're really good at it," he added wickedly before disappearing back down into the bowels of the boat, a large spanner clutched in one of his grimy hands.

Well, I pumped and pumped and pumped. Eventually the thing began to resemble a collection of fat half hoops, joined together with lengths of weighted chain covered in rust. By the time I got to the fat tube at the end, it covered most of the deck.

A short chap in a dark blue wetsuit appeared at my side just as the lowering black wreck of a castle came into view as we rounded a rocky headland. The engines were suddenly cut and the ensuing silence engulfed our gently bobbing craft. A small rowing boat quietly drew alongside and the coils of rubber were carefully tipped into the water. There was a splash as the thing hit the dancing wavelets and after a hurriedly whispered conversation, the man in the wetsuit dived into the gloomy depths to reappear further out, dragging the glistening hoops behind him. I hurriedly inflated the last bit of rubber and tossed it down into the rowing boat. It had an odd shape, a bit like a laughing horse.

Clarris came and sat down beside me. She was nursing a large steaming mug and tittering.

"What's up?" I asked.

"Look," she whispered, pointing out towards the other side of the Loch. Following her finger I suddenly saw a creature I had only ever heard about in books. The long black neck dipped with the swelling breeze and the curving snake-like coils tapered off into the swirling eddies of milk-white water vapour.

"Argh! It's the Loch Ness Monster," I squawked.

"Yep. The same one you've spent hours blowing up."

"What?"

"Edwin, just where is it you keep the spare brain cell?"

"Normally he just sits on it like most men," Mavis scoffed, sitting down on my other side. "Impressive, huh?" she added, pointing to the creature now bobbing further out to our left.

"Apparently they do this every day except on Sundays, Bank Holidays and the day after Charlie's birthday," she added, nibbling on a biscuit.

"Who do?" I asked, totally lost.

"The crew. The tourist board pay them to tow Nessie around, either at sunset or sunrise for about an hour, depending on the tide and the weather. Then they deflate her, pack her up and toddle off to the nearest pub."

"Why?"

"For the tourists, dummy."

"But ..."

"Everyone likes a good monster story, the hotels and pubs rely on Nessie turning up at regular intervals to keep the holidaymakers and monster-hunters coming back each year and think of the number of soft toys you can sell after a really good sighting."

"A good sighting?"

"Yeah, just imagine that you are a lone tourist sitting out on a rock near the castle. When, at the eerie sound of a bagpipe being molested by the brawny hand of some strong rugby-thighed Scotsman in a bottom-hugging kilt you spot the dark head of some prehistoric beast merging just as suddenly back into the dark swirls and white crests of the famously haunted loch."

"But ..."

"I mean you thought it was real, and you'd blown it up!" Mavis added, not even bothering to keep a straight face.

"But ..."

"But what?" Clarris asked.

"What about the real one?"

Clarris and Mavis both laughed until their sides hurt and Mavis threatened to do a puddle. They even told old Charlie, who it turned out was the midget in the wetsuit. I gritted my teeth and let them as I helped Murdock and Pete deflate the long, wet and oily coils of rubber.

They had clearly not seen what I'd seen – a slightly

quizzical head had been watching us from the ivy and shrub-curtained gloom of the cliffs supporting the skeletal remains of Urquhart castle. And considering the stick I'd get if I told, they certainly wouldn't hear about it now.

They were still chuckling as we landed just outside the white-painted outskirts of Inverness and trudged up from the landing stage towards Fort George.

chapter thirty-two

The madness of Prince George

We tramped, our knapsacks on our back, past the glowing outskirts of Inverness and carried on along the pathway running alongside the main road for what seemed like hours. It isn't until you are walking along a Scottish B road in the dead of night without the aid of a torch, that you realize what true silence is. It's soft and in my view invariably wet. The air smelt of leaves and wet dogs, heavily laced with cooling tarmac and the odd sprinkling of chip wrappers.

Every hour we'd stop and Murdock would look at a scrap of paper he had secreted in one of his many pockets, mutter to himself and then we'd have a quick drink and a sugary tablet which tasted of Horlicks and we'd be off again, shouldering our packs and trying not to walk on the burst bits of our blisters. At least Mavis and Clarris had acquired a pair of trainers each or we'd never have managed to get to the hinterland of Inverness, let alone past it.

Every so often a truck or lorry would pass us and we'd all flatten ourselves into the side and stare into the woods or field beyond, so the drivers and passengers wouldn't spot the reflective glints of our eyes. This was a tip passed on by Pete, who had overnight turned from an old friend into the SAS version of Captain Sensible.

The first rays of the newly rinsed sun were just beginning to crawl along the purple and pink ribbons of dawn when we finally got within spitting distance of our goal, the impregnable Fort George.

Apart from the sign saying 'Fort George 2 miles', I'd begun to notice that the only vehicles that had passed us for some considerable time were green and had camouflage-painted canvas sides and tops. It wasn't the sort of observation I was deeply happy about.

As soon as the traffic began to build up, we began to run along the edge of the road and at the first sound of an oncoming engine would flatten ourselves into the nearest ditch or patch of cover. By the time we eventually got near enough to actually see the fort, we were uniformly covered in dirt, sand and bits of foliage. We were also tired, hungry and very thirsty.

Pete, who appeared to have taken over temporary leadership, led the way through a tall patch of bracken which led down to a gravel and sand beach. We sheltered in the shadowed lee of a large rock while Murdock and Pete conversed together in short, soft, whispered sentences.

After a while Murdock nodded and crept away into the growing light. Pete muttered something to Clarris who also nodded, I thought rather reluctantly, and then he too stealthily crept away out of sight. Mavis, Clarris and I waited and waited, until finally we gave up and went to sleep, taking it in turns to play guard dog.

It was gone midday when Murdock and Pete returned, within minutes of each other, both looking equally depressed. Murdock had a large carrier bag which contained a variety of pies and crisps, together with five cans of Coke and a bag of extra strong mints.

We sat on various slabs of cold stone on the other side of the rock, to avoid being seen from the fort, which in broad daylight was clearly an impressive and well-maintained stockade.

"He's in there all right," Pete admitted, gloomily biting into a pasty.

"Aye, and he's very heavily guarded twenty-four hours a day by what I could see," Murdock agreed, taking a can and ripping the ring-pull off with his teeth.

"They seem to change guards at eight in the morning and then again at eight in the evening, according to the chap that delivers the bread." Pete scowled darkly and kicked a stone with his foot.

"Well, that's it then, we couldn't get in there with a small army and a couple of tanks."

"Not necessarily." Murdock gave Mavis an oddly secretive look and then stared intently down into the bottom of his crisp packet. "There might be a way of getting close to the Young Pretender."

There was a short thoughtful silence broken by Pete who belched loudly and then after a burst of red-faced apologies finally said, "Do tell."

"He's going to give a press conference at three o'clock – there's a notice on the wall next to the sentry box and I saw a couple of reporters milling around looking fed up to the back teeth."

"Which means he's letting them all in as a group, one or two more not making that much of a difference," Pete mused, looking as if the same devious idea had just hit the old grey cells.

Mavis, who had been aimlessly watching a cormorant diving for fish out in the sea beyond our sheltering cliff, turned and fixed them with a pair of fairly baleful eyes. "So what is it exactly that you want me to do as I'm the only one with a genuine press pass?"

"Nothing much, you just go in, take a seat, listen to what he has to say, make a few notes, be your usual vitriolic self and then leave. Simple enough, right?"

"Wrong," Mavis hissed. "How am I supposed to be my normal self looking like this?"

"No problem, all you need is some clean clothes, including that belt you call a skirt and a bit of lick and spit. I've got a packet of baby wipes somewhere." Murdock began to rummage through his backpack until he found the small plastic sachet of thin wet wipes, which were handed over, together with a hairbrush and a small phial which turned out to be a compact travelling toothbrush complete with toothpaste.

Mavis grumbled as she and Clarris moved to a more private bit of rock, returning with a scowling but very clean Mavis. It was then that I had my bright idea.

"I could go too," I announced. "As the photographer. I've got a camera, bought it in Oban."

I looked around at the uniformly stony faces.

"Out of the question!" Clarris uttered between clenched, deeply disapproving lips.

Mavis bit her own lip in a thoughtful fashion and then asked, "Show me the camera."

Carefully I extracted my miniature pride and joy from the pocket of my coat.

"Old Ted has one like this," she grudgingly stated as she handed it back.

"You know, it would look a lot better if I had company and everyone knows I never go anywhere without a lens handy for those extra special unplanned-for moments." She grinned, remembering some of the better ones.

Pete and Murdock shifted uncomfortably.

"Well, he's scruffy enough for a photographer," Pete admitted.

"Still …" Murdock stuttered, unsure about the wisdom of letting me anywhere near our quarry.

"I forbid it, I absolutely forbid it!" Clarris snorted, blowing a gasket.

Pete threw me the remaining baby wipes and Murdock extracted a clean shirt from the collection of items stowed away in his cavernous bag.

Ten minutes later Mavis and I stumbled onto the main road, she in her heels and eye-boggling skirt and me in my newly acquired wraparound shades and baggy shirt.

As we neared the throng surrounding the first of the many guard posts, I realized that I was finally doing something I had actually volunteered for. It was a brief warm fuzzy feeling which vanished the moment we reached the first of many inquisitors.

"Name?" A tall guard in full battle dress barked.

"Mavis Wordsworth," Mavis announced in a slightly peeved voice, giving the distinct impression that to not recognize her put the guard in the same family bracket as bacteria.

"You are not on my list," he announced, glaring at her.

"Not on your list? Of course I'm not on your list. But would any self-respecting journalist such as myself miss such an opportunity as this, for a good dig at the establishment? I don't think so."

The guard looked at her again and then as wisdom slowly dawned, said in slightly friendlier tones, "You're not that Mavis Wordsworth?"

"Indeed I am."

"You did that bit on the Minister for Transport and the love eggs, that time she got stuck in security at Heathrow and they had to call the army in."

"One of my best – to this very day I still get letters about it."

"I bet you do," he breathed admiringly, now taking in the lip gloss, black kohl-lined eyes and the fact that if he bent over a bit he could see all the way down the front of her blouse to her navel.

"Who's the accessory?" he asked in a much quieter voice.

"Photographer. Some local hick from the college, all I could manage at short notice," she replied, running the wet tip of her tongue around the top of her red shiny lips.

"Pass," the soldier announced and then said as an aside as we did just that, "I get off at eight."

"I'll bear that in mind." Mavis slouched seductively off and wiggled her way to the next checkpoint.

"Tart," I muttered as we did the same thing with the next three guards. We were nearly outfoxed at the last sentry box though, as the chap there took absolutely no notice of her whatsoever. He was about to remove us bodily from the waiting group who were now beginning to move around like a large and hungry school of great white sharks, when on a sudden inspired impulse I whispered in my softest campest undertone that Mavis was a complete bitch and never replied to any invitations, which was probably why we weren't on his list. I then let him know that she was also the most accomplished slut I'd ever met and that it would do her good to be frogmarched to the nearest door and thrown out on her tight little behind but that I'd probably lose my job and that my dear old Mum would be really upset. Mavis stood in stunned silence as I pouted, wriggled and shrugged.

But it worked and he let us in on the understanding that I met him for a drink at some club nearby, called the 'Side door'.

"Tart – you actually called me a tart you, you …" I blinked at her and wiggled the shades now squarely perched on the bridge of my nose. "Bitch!" she finished, and then with a toss of her head marched off towards the room where our fellow carnivores were circling in earnest.

We sat at the back clutching our courtesy clipboard and press packs. Several people glided by and muttered brief words of acknowledgement, tinged with a few morsels of salacious gossip. Most thought that she'd either been in Europe still on the hunt for my alter ego or on holiday, both scenarios causing no undue interest at all.

Finally, after most of us had settled into our seats and had begun to look bored, there was a fanfare of trumpets from the speakers in the ceiling and Warwick and a couple of oversized gym fanatics, dressed in black trousers and dark purple polo shirts with gold epaulettes, entered the room.

"Good afternoon, ladies and gentlemen of the press. As you know I have called this meeting to enable you to be able to meet and talk to the future king of Scotland, His

Royal Highness, Prince George. Would you all please stand for his …" Warwick looked around at the assembled group and then flexed his neck and hissed like an enraged swan.

"I said, would you all please stand." On the word 'stand' he grabbed the gun of the soldier standing next to him and fired into the ceiling. Bits of glass and polystyrene rained down on the frozen members of the press still sitting down, the others, having had some experience of reporting from a war zone, had already dived for cover under their seats. Slowly we all stood up and moved as a body closer to the back of the room.

"That's better," Warwick observed, grinning at us.

"All that tosser needs is a glass of Chianti and a plate of beans and he could impersonate Hannibal Lector better than that welsh git Hopkins," the hack beside me hissed through clenched teeth.

I was by now beginning to be seriously scared, that is until the short and skinny form of the future king arrived in person. He was quite possibly the most unprepossessing and least likeable human being I had ever laid eyes on. For a start he looked a bit like an anorexic Hitler, complete with daft moustache and bad skin. His eyes continually darted around the room and he fiddled with various parts of his body most of the time. But as soon as he opened his mouth and spoke I knew that it had just got a lot worse. Every word was poisoned from within by the sort of self-obsessed rhetoric that normally lives within the confines of some of the nastier award-winning plays. His voice grated and the shuffling gait and hunched shoulders did nothing to lessen the general feeling of mass loathing which was beginning to emanate from my fellow listeners.

For an hour and a half we were shown videos and stills

depicting the new order interspersed with the slightly insane ramblings of one of the dafter and most dangerous fruitbats I'd ever come across. Mavis made a few notes in the margin of her board but as the tirade against women, the establishment, socialists, communists and any group ending in an 'ist' grew, I began to wonder fleetingly if we were ever going to get out of the room either sane or more importantly, alive.

At the end of the talk we were invited to ask questions. There was a deathly hush. Finally a portly man in brown tweed stuck his hand up and gulped. "Um. You said you want to become head of the church and that you want to stop women from becoming ordained?"

"Yes."

"Well, don't you think that that might upset the ladies who have already been ordained and are in fact doing a very good job; take the Archbishop Gladys Cuthbertson …"

The Prince had gone puce with rage and the portly gent faltered in mid-flow and stared helplessly at the podium.

"If women want to continue in the church they marry vicars or join a convent. A woman can't be trusted with the Lord's work, their mandate is to produce children and if they can't, to abase themselves before God and man. Is God a woman? I don't think so. But I do know this, I know that I have been called to be the earthly representative of the divine and I will represent that godhead to the last breath in my body. For too long have we suffered the tyranny of women and the nanny state, no more will we tremble at the sound of some well-meaning social worker who extols us to understand. No longer will our jobs be taken by some woolly-haired Mecca-bowing darkie with shifty eyes. Let us give this land back to the true inheritors of the old Norse gene, let Scotland be run by the Scottish man and let England be run by the English man." He balled his hand into a fist and almost goose-stepped across the stage.

Uneasily I poked Mavis in the ribs and rolled my eyes towards the exit. Careful not to make a sound, we edged our way to the back wall and on the pretext of desperately needing the bathroom we made it to the end of the corridor. We could hear loud shouting from the room we'd just left and our instinct to survive now on full red alert, dived into a small cupboard containing a variety of cleaning utensils.

We waited in the semi-darkness until we heard the hurried approach of many feet. Quietly we emerged from our hiding place and joined a subdued band of fellow hacks. They were all discussing the interview in hushed tones and all of them without exception were agreeing with the lunatic we'd just seen. Frowning, I stepped heavily on Mavis's foot just as she looked set to argue back.

One of them asked her what she thought, to which she replied with a shrug that she wasn't bothered as she was getting married anyway and she was pregnant. Suitably satisfied, the group turned towards the door leading to the grass verges outside. It was as we felt fresh air on our faces that we heard the sound of gunshots and screams. Horrified, we walked even more quickly to the next checkpoint and after we had reached the final one set off at a fast trot away from the guards and the ever-moving cameras and lights.

We were almost at the main road when the others joined us. A bus stood at the corner whilst the driver, a flat cap over his head, snored gently in his seat. Mavis and I flung ourselves up the steps, threw a handful of notes at the shelf marked 'Pay and stay all the way' and sank into separate baggy seats. We were so relieved to be out of the claustrophobic atmosphere and away from those final terrified screams that we hadn't even noticed whether or not Murdock, Pete and Clarris had done the same thing.

When we got to the central bus depot at Inverness, we disembarked and stood trembling at the side of the road.

"I need a drink," Mavis demanded, and without waiting for a reply headed off in the direction of the nearest bar.

chapter thirty-three

Coming of age

Mavis sat hunched over her pint as if it would suddenly grow legs and walk away. She hadn't said anything at all for ten minutes, which was on par with Murdock giving up alcohol or the Pope wearing pink.

"So what happened?" Pete finally asked after Mavis had managed to imbibe most of the glass's contents in record time.

Mavis said nothing at all.

"Oh come on love, it couldn't have been that bad," Murdock mumbled, giving her a friendly rub on the shoulder.

"Oh couldn't it?" she finally snapped and then very slowly she took a small black object from the inside pocket of her jacket and laid it on the table. Expertly she flicked a tiny red-lit button and the uppercrust tones of Mr Warwick hovered above the table.

The silence that accompanied the next half hour or so was almost palpable, the only sound being either Mavis or myself getting up to get another round in or sitting down with the refilled glasses.

When the last sobbing scream had faded, Mavis sat back and deliberately lit and smoked one of Pete's hand-rolled specials.

"Good God," Clarris finally said, breaking the silence.

"He's completely nuts," Mavis murmured. "He's also got about ten thousand similar minded, chauvinist, sexist, racist pigs behind him according to a reporter from the *Dorset Herald*."

"He must have the entire membership of every dodgy fascist society and their illegal firepower behind him as well," Pete added, shaking his head in disbelief.

"Are you honestly going to tell me that he's going to get any real support from anyone? He's a barmpot!" Clarris screeched, slamming down her drink.

I got another round in while Clarris and Mavis verbally pulled him to pieces and like two terriers with a dead rabbit they were still at it when I got back.

"So Edwin, you were there, what do you think?" Murdock asked, an odd glint in his eye.

"Well …" I sat deep in thought for about ten seconds. I could lie and I'd just about get away with it, on the other hand … "If I hadn't met you, Clarris, and I was still working in the IT pool, being picked on by my manager, that fat cow Betty Allbright, and then going home to Mum because I couldn't afford a flat – you know the sort of thing, forget to wipe your muddy feet and it's clean out the toilet with a toothbrush, no holidays or nipping down to see the football because it's full of nasty men spitting at each other, being last in the queue at the chippie because I'm not the right ethnic mix, I'm just white, male, have a dead-end job, no wife, no kids and I'm under twenty-five, well then …"

They sat and looked at me as if finally seeing the real Edwin Snipe.

"I'd bloody well join him."

Murdock sat back and grinned at me, Pete goggled and Mavis looked horrified. Clarris, on the other hand, actually appeared to be listening.

"I'm not an intellectual and I don't know what it was like before the New Management. A government is a government whoever sits in the driving seat. I really don't care as long as at the end of the day I get paid a fair wage for doing a dead-end job and living in a dead-end street, where the only excitement is whether or not Mr Patil from across the road will manage to keep his wife of ten years away from his mistress of eight who lives on the other side of the cement works and works as a supply teacher for my mother. What I don't want is someone in charge of my life who not only acts and talks like my mum but actually believes it's in my best interests. And maybe, just maybe, I actually enjoy eating the wrong things and drinking the wrong things and staying up late. So yes, if it came to the crunch I'd vote for the turd, especially as it's a billion to one chance against my ever really meeting him, or for that matter ever really wanting to. After all, what do I have to lose and by what yardstick can you possibly persuade me that it's wrong? I'm a man, which means I'm a second-class citizen from the moment my balls dropped. I'm white, which means that if there aren't enough ethnic minority representatives in my department I get moved sideways, demoted or sacked and all of this has nothing whatsoever to do with me. I don't go to church so why the hell should I care who gets to sit at the top table? I don't own any land, so it really doesn't matter to me whether half the country is in the hands of the state or some aristocratic throwback, after all I still pay the same amount of rent. If we do go back to some glorified Victorian society why should I complain – I'm a man, I've got to be better off somewhere along the line, haven't I?"

Mavis opened her mouth to say something but then closed it again and handed me a cigarette. I lit it and took a long hard pull. It was perhaps the second most disgusting thing I'd ever had in my mouth, with the possible exception of a 'Murdock special'. Hastily I stabbed it out in the ashtray and took a gulp of beer to ease the taste.

"So," Clarris said, thoughtfully studying my face, "what our friend Warwick has is a puppet who will appeal to the lowest common denominator white male."

"Yes."

"Then I have to see someone. Pete, can you give Argyll a call?"

Pete nodded and sauntered off. He returned just as the shout of 'last orders' ricocheted around the optics and with a nod towards the exit indicated that we ought to leave. He waited on the corner until we'd emerged from the main doors and with a brief whistle marched off down a narrow, brick-walled side alley. We followed in a straggling single file as he led us in and out of alleys and cobbled streets flanked by rows of terraced houses. Eventually we reached the outskirts of Inverness where the larger detached residences hid behind broad sweeping drives and tree-fringed security fences.

Finally, just when I was about to lay down on the nearest bit of dry pavement and sleep for a week, he gave a low whistle and stopped.

chapter thirty-four

The conspirators

There was a man waiting for us at the end of the road. Or at least I presumed it was a man; if it wasn't then it was one very tall, thin lady. Pete paused as the figure moved from the shadows of a high stone wall and then started in recognition as it moved nearer. Murdock, sensing some possible conflict, drew us away from the direct light of an overhead streetlamp and we waited.

I'd managed to chew two fingernails down to the quick before Pete returned.

"Come on," he hissed, "and for God's sake be quiet, it's not safe."

At the word's 'not safe' part of me slunk further inwards and another part just got angry. The angry part scowled and followed Pete, who led the way across the road, through a tall gated driveway and into the back of what appeared to be a garden shed. The thin shape was already there, pulling old clay flowerpots and sacking away from the centre of the floor. After the last compost-stained item had been removed, a trapdoor was revealed, which when opened led the eye down towards a flight of crumbling, dank stone steps.

Carefully we approached the pit and one by one felt our way to the bottom. With a feeling of déjà vu and expecting at any moment to be jovially slapped on the back by the Growler, I followed the body in front along a low-roofed tunnel, which dripped far more ominously than anything we'd passed through in the *Maybole Rose*.

All this was done in the cold darkness of my own worst nightmare, so much so that when a door in the wall at the end was opened to reveal a vast well-lit cellar filled from floor to ceiling with dark brown metal-rimmed barrels and no gangster clones wielding large semi-automatics, I breathed an audible and shaky sigh of relief.

We stood in a shivering queue and waited for something to happen. After a couple of minutes nothing had, so we finally began to move around a bit.

"Murdock?" I asked, peering at the casks.

"What?"

"Why do all these barrels have 'Jerez' written on them? I mean, isn't that Spanish for sherry?"

"Sherry barrels give the national drink its golden colour," stated a strange voice behind me. I jumped about two feet and landed facing a middle-aged lady in a smart lavender wool suit and matching shoes. She was also carrying a handbag in the same shade of lavender in one hand and a small silver polished revolver in the other.

"So," she asked, watching us, a half-smile playing on her thin carmine lips. "Which one of you is Edwin Snipe?"

"I am," I replied, waiting for the inevitable gunshot.

There was a moment of silence and then slowly and carefully she put the gun away in her handbag and took my arm.

"Well then, young man, I expect you want something to

eat, before we give you a lift."

Eat? lift? I hadn't got a clue what was going on but the weaponry had been stashed so things could only get better, or at least that's what the optimistic side of me hoped. The resident pessimist, on the other hand, wanted to find the nearest bathroom and hide in the toilet.

We were then escorted through another door, up a flight of steps and into a large panelled hallway. There were old frayed rugs on the floor and some real oil paintings on the wall, one depicting a large man sitting on a rock cradling a long gold rifle, a dog panting at his feet with a brightly feathered but very dead bird in its mouth.

At the end of the hall a huge fire glowed and crackled in a fireplace the size of my bedroom and a man sitting in a tall, high-backed leather chair in front of it got up and slowly made his way towards us. As he moved nearer I realised that he was the man in the picture. He was a little older, thinner and frailer, judging by the noise that his metal-tipped stick made as it tap-tapped its way across the floor in front of him.

"So you're Toby's son?" he announced, watching me from blue-veined and hooded eyes.

"Come and sit down. Evelyn my dear, please tell cook that there will be five extra at dinner."

"Yes dear." The woman in the lavender suit moved back down the hall and vanished behind another door set into the dark wood panelling.

"You look very like him," the old man announced. "Sit down all of you," he barked as he lowered himself back down into the cushioned seat of his own chair.

A cat the colour of striped toffee crept from under the chair legs and launched itself at the old man's lap, where it was stroked until it curled into a small fluffy ball and purred loudly, its large, malevolent yellow eyes finally closing.

"He said you would come," the man announced, sitting back and regarding me earnestly over long fingers steepled together in front of his chin.

"Oh," I replied, trying desperately hard to think of something intelligent to say.

"I presume you got his message?" the man asked, ignoring everyone else but me.

"What message?" I asked.

The man sat further back and then dropped his gaze from me to the fire.

"I must say I'd rather assumed you would have brought the answer with you."

"What answer?"

"The answer to our joint problem. Yours and mine. Otherwise why did you bring her?" He pointed to Clarris with a bony index finger.

"Clarris."

"Yes, the heir apparent, the lady in waiting."

"Er ..." I hadn't got a clue what he was going on about, and helplessly I turned to Clarris for guidance but she was staring intently at a large picture of a lady with very little on at all, except for a small piece of cloth the size of a man's handkerchief and even that was see-through.

"She came of her own accord," Murdock answered.

"Oh, and who are you?"

"Murdock, although you may have heard of me by my professional name."

"Which is?"

"The Scorpion."

I stared at Murdock in total disbelief – what the hell was

going on? 'The Scorpion'? I thought Murdock was just a mad extremely rude cartoonist but now he sounded like the hit man of an old Jack Higgins plot. The old man, however, laughed outright and held out his right hand, which Murdock moved towards and calmly shook.

"The scorpion. Oh yes, I have heard of you. Do they know that you are still alive?" he asked, eyes glittering with sudden merriment.

"I doubt it, it's been a long time."

"But old habits die hard, eh?"

"Old habits never die, your Lordship."

" I see."

Well I didn't and from the look on Mavis's face neither did she. However, we appeared to be the only ones who didn't.

I coughed loudly and when I had everyone's attention said, in what were for me extremely chilly tones, "Would anyone care to enlighten me as to when my mushroom status will cease?"

Mavis gave a small titter.

"Mushroom status?" the old man muttered querulously.

"Yes, you know. They keep you in the dark, cover you in shit and then cut your legs from under you."

The old man glared at me and then laughed out loud, a great deep bark of amusement.

"Ah young Edwin, you really are like old Toby."

There was another pause in which Evelyn returned to stand silently behind the old man's chair.

"I suppose you had better know. I thought you would be bringing with you the invention that your father developed and which I believe finally killed him. The man that orchestrated your father's death is at this very moment settling an army of malcontents and mercenaries around him and the day after tomorrow intends to have himself crowned King of all Scotland. He will then march on London and declare himself king there too." There was a brief pause before he continued, his voice heavy with bitter resentment. "He will abolish both governments and also crown himself Lord High Protector of the Church of England, Scotland, Wales and Ireland. Women will be demoted and thrown out of every position of authority and women priests will be cast from the body of the church. He will also take back all the land which used to be owned by the Crown and will in all honesty cause more bloodshed and sorrow than either Lord Cromwell or King Charles the First put together."

"So where do I come in?" I whispered, the gravity of the situation finally hitting me between the eyes.

"You?"

"Yes."

"Well, I thought you had come up here to assassinate your father's killer, using the very thing which your father died trying to protect. But it appears that Toby protected it too well."

"Not necessarily," Murdock announced, moving away from the fire.

"You have a plan?"

"Well, Pete and I do but we need to have a package delivered to us by tomorrow night and we need to get into the robing room before the Prince."

"Anything else?"

"Yes, we need to persuade young Edwin here to act as bait."

"Bait!" I managed to squeak.

"No!" Clarris boomed, rising from her chair. "Edwin has

done enough. I won't allow him to be used any more."

Not allow, not …

"That's fine by me," I announced, standing abruptly. The cat opened an eye and glared at me.

"Just tell me where and when, but first I could eat a horse."

Murdock and Pete laughed but Mavis and Clarris looked at me as if I'd just sprouted two heads and neither of them was particularly attractive. Frankly I'd reached the point of no return, that point where Macbeth had twittered on about it being just as hard to go back as to go on. He'd tied it all up with rivers and blood and stuff but I'd finally got the general idea. I didn't much fancy a world run by some macho lunatic who thought he was God and I liked the idea of him being aided and abetted by that slimy git Warwick even less … and if it meant standing my ground like some poor old tethered donkey waiting for the lion then so be it.

chapter thirty-five

'D' Day

We spent the rest of the following day being driven southwards by a completely mute member of his Lordship's staff. The vehicle was an exceptionally comfortable peoplecarrier with darkened windows and some of the nicest seats I'd sat on for a long time. It also didn't smell of fish, decomposing vegetable matter or old socks.

We arrived in Edinburgh just before teatime and were bustled quietly into a tall stone-faced tenement which backed onto an area Murdock referred to as the Golden Mile.

Pete and Murdock spent their time twitching the dirty net curtains at the front window and whispering to each other. I, on the other hand, found an old copy of a classic Ian Rankin and disappeared into the bathroom where I stayed immersed up to my shoulders in peaty water until I resembled a stewed prune, that is until Clarris banged on the door to let me know that dinner was ready. I continued to read at the table, which was studiously ignored, and then hurried off to bed with a mug of some hot malted drink to find out what happened at the end.

The following morning Clarris woke me with a soft and warmly loving kiss, which was, I have to admit, thoroughly reciprocated and after a quick breakfast she and Mavis bundled me out of the door and up a long, brightly-lit cobbled street, towards the towers and dour green granite walls of Edinburgh Castle, which loomed out of a swathe of frigid, cold grey mist hanging malignantly over the city of Edinburgh.

Everywhere we went there were men in uniform either cleaning, holding or posing with some form of armament. People hurried by and as we neared the entrance to the castle, the crowds thickened and began to belly out, wedging the soldiers in behind the long, thick, red and gold coils of rope which were being used as barriers by the police.

At the stroke of ten the doors to the castle were flung open and to a fanfare of trumpets, held this time by a band of teenage youths, the soon-to-be-crowned King emerged in a flurry of rich red velvet and ermine-trimmed cape.

Murdock and Pete, who had made their way through the crowds to stand beside us, squinted down at their watches. Murdock frowned and looked up at the clouded sky.

"Have you any idea how long it takes to work?" he asked.

"No idea. We soaked the stuff pretty well but it's not tweed."

"Why the bloody hell couldn't he have left a few instructions?" Murdock grumbled.

"Oh shit, that's blown it," Pete groaned. A long, black, smoky-glassed limousine had pulled up and a few dark-suited men had got out and were approaching the smiling waving heir apparent. I watched as he was led, still smiling and waving, to the waiting car.

"If he gets in we've had it," Murdock muttered. "No one will see and Warwick will just find another patsy. You would think that the little swine could at least walk to the Cathedral?"

I stared from one to the other and then to Clarris who was standing beside me looking pale and suddenly very frail. Whatever their grand plan was, it had failed, according to Murdock because they needed more time.

Time.

The minutes and the hours that Warwick had taken from my father, those few precious seconds that might have led to the start of some sort of resolution between a man I'd never really met and the part of me that had never known who I really was.

Time, and a lot of lies – well perhaps it was time for a few more and as Mavis said 'if you dressed it in a little bit of truth it could run on for months'.

"He's not the real king!" I shouted, pushing myself from the crowd. Soldiers began to emerge in front of me, brandishing their weapons.

"Is this what you want?" I asked, projecting my voice as I'd never been able to do in any of my school plays. "A puppet king and him pulling the strings?" I pointed to Warwick who was beginning to shuffle ever so slowly back towards the castle.

"Do you honestly think that you are going to be better off with this lot?" I screamed.

"Do you really want to know what they do to people who don't agree with them?" There was a growing silence and the cameras that had flashed as I burst from behind the taut ropes went into manic overdrive.

"They get their paid private army to shoot them until they stop moving!" I screamed.

"Nonsense! Somebody stop him," Prince George shouted. A soldier ran towards me; it was my friend from the previous day and a bead of sweat dribbled down his forehead as he looked down the red cross of his gunsight straight into my eyes.

"Do you think he's going to allow you to do what you like? Anyone, anyone who doesn't conform will be punished."

"That's not true! You all want to get rid of the socially pliable ethnic pigs that run this country, the ones always with their snouts in the trough."

"And what about the homosexuals?"

"Those degenerates, those abominations against God it says in the Bible …"

The rifle was slowly lowered and I saw several others moving to stand with the crowd, rather than facing them.

"My father's gay and so are his friends and I don't want him put up against a wall and shot or imprisoned. You want a return to Victorian values? You really want that?" I asked, my voice thickening with an emotion I hadn't really known I'd felt until then. "Child labour and prostitution, that's what we could return to. Ladies, do you want your twelve-year-old working in some brothel servicing old men who beat their wives, never see their children and abuse their servants? Well, do you?"

There was now a distinct murmur from the crowd.

"All I want is to get back to a few family values," the heir apparent shrieked, his face twisted in what had started out as a false grin and was turning into uncontrollable rage.

"Family values! What the bloody hell would you know

about family values? Your family wouldn't know what they were if you sent them on a two-week refresher course with St Peter himself!"

Someone laughed and the mass of people around us began to edge forwards.

"Shoot him!" the Prince demanded, shaking visibly, the ermine now beaded in angry sweat.

"What, like you shot old Edward Airedale from the *Caledonian*?" A deep voice shouted from the crowd. "He did, you know, I was there – I had to say I'd support the mad bastard just to stay alive. Old Eddie wouldn't though, silly brave old sod. So that skinny tyke had him murdered!" The invisible speaker continued, his voice rising hysterically.

The crowd began to slowly mutter and move even closer. A brick landed just past my feet and George stared at it as if mesmerized.

"But I'm your Prince. I'm God's chosen heir – I've come to bring you back to Him."

It was then that I remembered Toby had smoked ever so slightly about a second or so before bursting into flames and odd though it seemed, so was his royal nastiness.

"Oh no you're not," I shouted. This was it ... in for a penny in for a pound; I just hoped the big man upstairs was listening.

"You're not his chosen one but if you are, may God strike me down as I speak."

I knelt then and bowed my head, remembering how far bits of Toby's jacket had flown.

There was a brief pause and the sun, which had been temporarily hiding behind a cloud, burst into glorious light above our heads and with a flash of white and gold the heir apparent burst into flames.

Nobody moved and nobody screamed, we just watched in stunned silence. I could hear cameras clicking and the soft sound of a video camera recording the event for posterity or the ten o'clock news. The body of the flaming prince stood for a moment longer and then crumpled to the ground with a soft hiss, leaving nothing more than a small heap of charred remains. A woman did scream at that point and the amazing heat, which had forced everyone to back away as far as possible, began to abate.

A man in a black suit arrived with a fire extinguisher and covered the remaining ashes with a coat of white foam; someone in the crowd started to clap very slowly and then someone else began to sing 'Scotland the Brave' out of tune, not that anybody cared. As they were just getting into the swing of the first chorus, I was grabbed from behind and manoeuvred towards the steep slope which eventually led around the sides of the cliff and down towards the Grassmarket.

Soon Murdock and Pete were reliving the whole thing and Mavis was adding in extra journalistic embroidery. Clarris tucked her hand in mine, and breathing a huge sigh, snuggled up next to me, her own individual scent rising in perfumed waves from soft, newly washed skin.

"You were amazing," she breathed, "absolutely amazing but if you ever pull a stunt like that again, I will personally throttle you with my bare hands."

chapter thirty-six

'Yes, Prime Minister'

A week later I received a personal invitation to meet the President at the Presidential Pink Palace. I bought a brand new suit for the occasion and looked, even I had to admit, a bit tasty, the result in no small part of my diet-free sabbatical, which had turned me into a more substantial and solid shape. Even Clarris seemed to approve of the new chunkier me.

Clarris stood beside me as the formal proceedings washed over my head; to be honest I was more interested in the six-course dinner I'd been promised than some award for services rendered.

At long last, just as my bottom was beginning to go numb from sitting on what could have been one of the most uncomfortable chairs I'd ever laid my Gluteus Maximus on, I was invited onto the podium to stand beside the President. The press began to shuffle forwards and several reporters stood to attention before a variety of monitors.

"This will be my last speech to you, the nation," the President began, taking a sip of water. Up close she was a lot smaller and older than I'd imagined and she had that wrinkled grey pallor of the very recently ill. "I have tried to lead you to the best of my ability but it is time to stand down and to let another younger person take my place." She turned and placed a tiny bony hand on Clarris's shoulder before re-addressing the assembled microphones and lenses. "I give you my successor … Edwin Snipe."

There was pandemonium. I stood, stunned, and stared over her smiling head to Clarris who was actually smiling back. I knew that smile and somehow, somewhere I had the distinct feeling I'd just been set up by the grandmaster of all set-ups.

It was then that the barrage started.

"Sir, how do you feel about being the first male President since the coming to power of the New Management?"

"Do you regret anything that you said in Edinburgh?"

"Are you going to set up better job opportunities for men?"

"Are you gay?"

"Do you believe, as the *Church Times* has stated, that you have a divine witness?"

"Do you intend to keep the old Cabinet on?"

"Are you going to control the press?"

"Will you be asking the House of Windsor back?"

And then some woman from *Hello* magazine asked the one question I had wanted to ask all week.

"Will you marry Clarris Sharpe?"

Clarris smiled down at her feet, and grabbing a small flower from the arrangement on the table behind us, I knelt suddenly and looked up at her, using my best puppy dog expression.

"Well, will you?" I asked. The press held their collective

breath.

"Will I what?" she asked, looking down at me.

"Marry me?"

"Yes."

The room exploded, and I was suddenly besieged from all sides.

Even the old President shed a glistening tear, although that might have been because I'd accidentally trodden on her foot while reaching for the flower.

Later after the six-course dinner, which was very good although to be perfectly honest I couldn't tell you what it was – I have a feeling there was a bit of fish because I got hollandaise on my tie – Clarris and I lay snuggled up in our newly decorated flat.

My old flatmates had gone to live across the hall and the spare rooms were slowly being turned into offices or at least one was; the other was having fluffy clouds painted on the ceiling.

"Clarris, do you really want me to be President?" I asked, nuzzling her ears.

"Of course."

"You don't mind?"

"Mind?"

"About me doing it rather than you."

"Edwin, it was my idea. How else do you think I got the Scots to agree to help Murdock and Pete get into the robing room?"

"What exactly was it they did?" I asked.

"Well you remember that you said you only had the one bag?"

"After Toby exploded?"

"Yes. Well Pete tracked it down to the police filing room

in Bournemouth and had it sent up to Edinburgh. Then he and Murdock tipped the entire contents of the bottles it contained onto Prince George's royal robes and then all we had to do was wait for the sun to come out. Unfortunately, because Toby didn't trust computers and left no records, we had absolutely no idea how long it would take to work."

"I know. I realized that when I tried to remember how long he'd been wandering around before he met me in the bookshop."

"Poor Toby. He wanted to invent a new kind of energy and invented a killing device instead."

"What will happen to his work?"

"Nothing. No one has the formula and the only chemicals he had left were used on that bastard of Warwick's. Besides, according to some of our best scientists it was totally unstable and had some sort of odd half-life. It also didn't react with ultraviolet light but some other wavelength and it has to be set off by strong sunlight. We have no idea which type of light and no way of making any more."

"Perhaps that's just as well."

"Darling?"

"Umm?" I began to nibble the inside of an earlobe whilst at the same time easing one hand under the bra cup of her dress.

"There's something I've got to tell you …"

"Yes …"

"About that night …"

"Which one …"

"The one after the row in Coventry."

"Oh, that one."

"Well, you remember what happened afterwards …"

Remember? I was at that precise moment trying to reenact it.

"I'm pregnant."

I stopped abruptly; that would certainly account for the fluffy clouds and the very small socks I'd discovered in her underwear drawer the other evening.

"You're going to have a baby?"

"That's what being pregnant usually means," Clarris sniffed, sitting up and regarding me much as someone would an unexploded bomb.

I was going to be a dad; I was actually going to be a dad.

"Does this mean that I don't have to be President?" I asked hopefully.

"No," was the short but succinct reply.

"Oh."

"One of us has to have a decent job."

"Right."

"I mean, have you any idea how much nappies cost? And clothes … and all those other things … like bottles and nipple protectors and …"

A week later I started on the new job. Nobody seemed to mind that I was a man, least of all the other members, who began to treat me as some sort of housetrained pet.

All sorts of things began arriving in the post from a variety of people. Including a box of kippers from the Manx Government.

And to be honest it wasn't a bad job and I was finally my own boss … just as long as I asked Clarris first.

Other books by Linda Mann published by Priory Press.
Please see our website for stockists and mail order:
www.priory-press.co.uk

Mr Boots

Fiona Harris is pleasantly surprised to become the sole beneficiary of her late Uncle's estate right up to the point when her newly acquired inheritance burns down in front of her very eyes and she learns from the local constabulary that her Uncle Quentin was murdered and she could be next.

The only clues she has are the names 'Anderson and Fiske' and the knowledge that it had something to do with her Uncle's seedy detective agency and a book about latter-day Resurrection Men.

Can she solve Uncle Quentin's last case or will she too swim with the fishes?

Set between Oban and Edinburgh Mr Boots features such over-the-top characters as

Mr Burke and Mr Hare – purveyors of bespoke assassinations at reasonable rates; Neville Foolscap – a failed writer and serial suicider; a doctor who doesn't like patients and a dead tax inspector who doesn't like anyone.

Mr Boots is based around a real ghost who allegedly lives under the South Bridge in Edinburgh; everything else is just my account of what happened after a well known reality television programme was filmed there – Linda Mann.

Mr Boots was full of fun and I happily whiled away a foray to Leeds in his company – Christopher Cook, writer /broadcaster

A very funny book – Bob Harrison, Manx Radio

This black comedy unravels a chilling tale of murder, revenge and mystery which starts on the shores of an ancient Scottish loch and ends in Edinburgh – Scottish Field Magazine, March 2006

The Corsican Trap

This is the third Tavistock Allan Mystery, a black comedy of murder, revenge and divers alarums set in the Isle of Man and in particular within the Victorian splendour of the Gaiety Theatre, Douglas.

Russell Gillings-Cooper is not a happy theatre manager for two very good reasons; not only does he have to deal with yet another amateur production of Noel Coward's improbable farce, 'Blithe Spirit' but the powers that be have dictated that the theatre be inspected by reality television's foremost ghost-hunter, Lou Sphinx. Not surprisingly the theatre ghosts are up in arms: someone is dressing up as the Phantom of the Opera and stealing anything not nailed to the floor and the plumbers have discovered a broken body behind the boiler.

Can Detective Brian Clague discover the culprit before the curtain goes up ion the first night?

Can-ex detective Bob Callow protect his first client Lou Sphinx from joining the increasing ranks of the recently deceased before he can submit his first invoice? Can Mannanan Mac Lir (minor deity third class, failed) make it as a civil servant working for the Department of Tourism and will Tavistock Allan actually manage to finish her next book without having to help out all of the above, including her husband Richard, who is attempting to direct and produce the aforementioned play?

A rollicking tale which brings together many of the characters from her previous books – Mist *and* The Tidemaster. *Full of thespian frailties and almost slapstick humour, it's a fun read – Manx Tails*, May 2007

A cross between Wodehouse, Dick Francis and Ben Elton … a very funny book –Phil & Co, Island Books, Manx Radio interview, 10 November 2006.

All books available by mail order from Priory Press Limited

Mr Boots	RRP £8.99
The Corsican Trap	RRP £8.99
The Chronicles of Edwin Snipe	RRP £8.99

Or purchase any three books for £20.00
Postage and packing free to the UK
For postage outside the UK please add £2.50

Please send a cheque to: New Orders Dept
Priory Press Ltd
Abbots Way
Abbotswood
Ballasalla
Isle of Man
IM9 3EQ

or visit our website www.priory-press.co.uk to pay direct